I0955202

WEST ★ TEXAS
SUNRISE

LONG ROAD TO LAROSA

A Novel

PAUL BAGDON

Published by Fleming H. Revell
a division of Baker Book House Company
P.O. Box 6287, Grand Rapids, MI 49516-6287
www.bakerbooks.com

Printed in the United States of America

Library of Congress Cataloging-in-Publication Data

Bagdon, Paul,
Long road to LaRosa / Paul Bagdon.
p. cm. — (West Texas sunrise ; bk. 2)
ISBN 0-8007-5815-3 (pbk.)
1. Sheriffs—Fiction. 2. Texas, West—Fiction. I. Title. II. Series: Bagdon, Paul. West Texas sunrise ; bk. 2.
PS3602.A39 L66 2003
813′.6—dc21 2002014648

This novel is dedicated, with thanks and love, to Peter Drago, Debbie DiPasquale, Mike Marini, Micheala Marini, Jackie Root, Cynthia Marini, and Paul LeBron. All of these people are the best friends a man could possibly have, and their importance to me is beyond the scope or power of mere words.

1

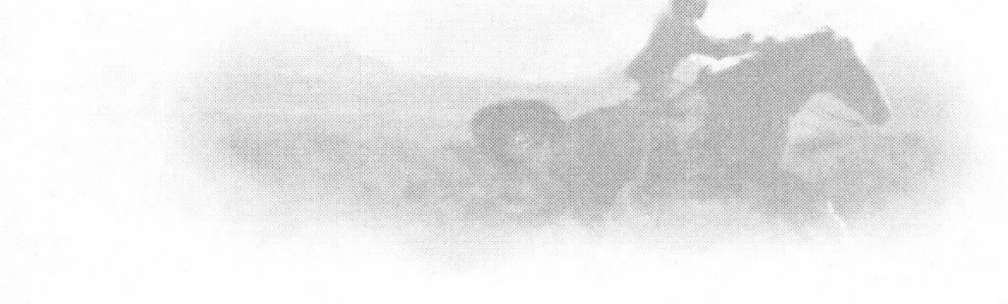

It was a magnificent day—a perfect day.

The dew on the scrubland and the patches of buffalo grass that spread endlessly around the path Lee Morgan rode made the earth sparkle and glitter in the early sun, turning it into a crystal fairyland. The air was still cool and so clean that it seemed as if the slightest clink of a stone against a steel horseshoe could carry clear and undistorted, bell-like, all the way across Texas and into Mexico.

Slick, Lee's prize stallion, seemed to be enjoying his day as well. His tongue toyed with the bit in his mouth, and he snapped up each hoof as soon as it struck the earth, dancing a bit sideways, snorting impatiently, wanting very much to run.

The fingers of Lee's left hand played the reins with the unconscious skill of a person who spends more hours in a saddle than out of it. She usually rode a stock saddle rather than the more demure and accepted sidesaddle, and she frequently wore culottes, which were similar to a man's trousers. Today was different, though. She wore a long dark skirt, high-buttoned shoes that pinched her feet, and a white blouse with feminine ruffles and a tightly buttoned collar. Her dark hair with its tones of auburn was twisted into a businesslike bun atop her head, rather than tumbling free past her shoulders as it usually did.

It was a day for formality, and Lee had acquiesced on her clothing. She needed the money, and she was quite sure Sam Turner, the founder and president of the Burnt Rock Land and Trust Company, was going to loan it to her. All she needed to do was sign the papers, and the money would be transferred to the operating account of her ranch, the Busted Thumb Horse Farm. She didn't like to borrow money, but a quarter horse breeder in Laramie was retiring, and she wanted to purchase four stallions and two broodmares for her string.

She took a long, deep breath and smiled as she exhaled. She was forty-one and had never been married, yet she'd devoted her life to raising the best, strongest, most intelligent ranch horses anywhere. Now with the almost-perfect Slick as a foundation stallion and the horses she'd receive from Laramie in a month, things couldn't be better.

The War Between the States had been over for a decade, and there had been rain—good, drenching rain—for the past three years. Her pastures were lush with knee-high grass. This year there'd been a crop of foals that were now fat and happy and playing in a fenced four-acre pasture just outside her back door.

Lee stood in the stirrups and looked at the prairie surrounding her, the scent of the fertile earth and the sweeter aroma of dewy grass and wildflowers touching her like a mother's caress. Yes, things couldn't be better.

Slick snorted wetly and shook his head, trying to get under the bit. Lee's hand went to her hair. She'd spent almost a half hour getting the bun to take shape and stay in place. Letting Slick run would make a mess of it. She centered her horse on the trail and rode at a sedate walk, feeling the tension in the muscles and sinews of the twelve-hundred-pound stallion. She touched her hair again and then sighed. Leaning forward a bit in the saddle, she let a foot of rein slide through her fingers and tapped her heels lightly against the gleaming ebony of Slick's side.

The horse exploded under her, all four hooves flinging clumps of dirt as he launched himself forward, digging for traction. His front legs reached far ahead of his body, dragging long yards of trail beneath him. He did what he did best—ran faster than any horse Lee had ever owned, ridden, or even seen in all her years. His gallop had the brutal power of an out-of-control steam locomotive, and she thrilled at his speed, as she did every time she let him run.

When she checked him and reined down to a lope, his chest and sides were wet with healthy sweat—and she imagined her hair looked like a haystack hit by a tornado. She stood in the stirrups, leaned forward, and kissed the horse between his ears.

What could go wrong on such a perfect day?

The first slug from the 44.40-caliber Sharp's buffalo rifle destroyed Sam Turner's right shoulder. The second round struck him lower, flaying off a strap of flesh and muscle four inches wide from the outer side of his right thigh. The almost-simultaneous impacts hurled him backward against the door of the safe behind his desk like a rag doll thrown by a cranky child. For a moment the silence in the Burnt Rock Land and Trust Company seemed like that of a sepulchre, as if the thunderous report of the rifle had assaulted all those in the bank, slamming them senseless and snatching away their ability to hear, to speak, to even understand what had just happened.

Then the moment was past. The two female clerks in their cages behind the counter screamed as senior teller Hiram Ruppert, in the cage between them, pawed for the Colt pistol Sam insisted he keep on a shelf next to his cash drawer. The handful of customers who'd been waiting in the tellers' lines dropped to the floor, covering their heads with their arms and bringing their knees to their chests.

Lee, who'd been walking toward Sam's desk with the signed loan agreement in her hand, moved before the others did. She took two quick steps toward Sam's sprawled, bloodied form, the paper floating from her hand to the floor. An outlaw moved into her path, grabbed her, and spun her around.

"You jist take it easy, sweet thing," he said, shoving her shoulder. She continued through the spin the man had started, with her left knee rising and her weight balanced on her right foot.

The outlaw's face collapsed as her knee slammed into his groin. He clutched himself with both hands and bent over. As his eyes rolled back, he dropped to the floor with his pistol under his inert body.

The man who appeared to be the leader blew a well-chewed plug of tobacco across the room as surprised laughter erupted from his mouth. He shook his head happily, looking Lee over. "I ain't leavin' this town without you, ma'am, an' that's for true," he promised, swinging the barrel of the Sharp's toward the male teller. "You want to die over some money that ain't even yours? Drop it!"

Hiram Ruppert met the outlaw's eyes for a moment, then looked away. The Colt struck the wooden floor with a thud. Two outlaws fanned out behind their leader, one covering the platform upon which Sam's desk and safe rested, the other covering the tellers' cages from his position at the entrance. Then the leader strode across the polished floor to Hiram's cage, the butt of the Sharp's still at his shoulder.

"Open the safe," he said.

"I don't know—"

"Tell me you don' know the combination and I'll blow your fool head off. Open the safe or die—it's nothin' to me to pull the trigger." The man's voice was conversational, as if he were simply asking a question about his account. His eyes, however, burned with intensity.

Hiram swallowed deeply. "I . . . I'll open it," he croaked.

The outlaw chuckled. "'Course you'll open it, you idjit. Don' make no sense to die for somethin' that ain't yours to begin with." He turned his head to wink at Lee. "You hold on there for a bit, honey. I'll be right with you."

Lee looked away and continued making her way to Sam's side. She knelt beside him and began peeling away his coat from his shoulder. She gasped when she uncovered the wound and saw the scraps of bone piercing his flesh. Blood gushed from the fist-sized opening in thick, glistening bubbles that broke and flowed to the floor.

The outlaw motioned Hiram toward the break in the counter. "Move," he said. His voice was no longer light.

Hiram's shoe struck the Colt on the floor as he moved from his position and eased past the sobbing tellers toward Sam's platform.

"Open it!" the outlaw snarled.

A short, muscular man poked his head through the entrance. "Zeb!" he called. "They're comin'! That lawman an' his deputy!"

"Good," the leader said with a grin, prodding Hiram with the barrel of his Sharp's. "The boys on the roof'll be right pleased about that."

Marshall Ben Flood's boots beat a dull rhythm on the wooden sidewalk as he ran from his office toward the bank, jacking a round into the chamber of his 30.30. He stumbled as a bullet from the bank roof splintered the dried wood directly in front of him. He caught his balance, snapped a shot toward the bank, levered his rifle again, and dove through the open door of Scott's Mercantile. Another round from the outlaws tore a palm-sized chunk of wood from the mercantile's door frame, inches over Ben's head. In a heartbeat, Nick Blake, his twenty-three-year-old deputy, hurled himself into the doorway, skidding across the floor on his stomach with his shotgun tucked lengthwise in his arms. The plate glass window exploded, launching splinters and shards of razorlike missiles into the front of the store.

"Everybody get behind something and keep down!" Ben shouted as he squirmed to the doorway and fired four rapid shots. The Sharp's roared again in response, its thunderous voice making the other weapons sound like cheap Fourth of July firecrackers. A dress form in the wreckage of the plate glass window spun into the store, a ragged hole the size of a skillet gaping in its chest.

Nick edged up next to Ben. "Lousy position," he grunted as he squeezed off a shot.

"For us, anyway. They're sittin' pretty. How many you think are on the roof?"

Nick fired again and a hoarse bellow of pain rose and ceased within the same instant. "One less than there was, but looks to be maybe eight or ten up there."

Ben sighted and squeezed off a round from his prone position on the floor. A tall, heavyset outlaw fell backward, and the barrel of his rifle caught the sun and glinted as it dropped from the rooftop to the ground.

Ben looked out at the street toward the bank. On the opposite side of the road, a beer wagon loaded with fifty-five-gallon wooden barrels was parked in front of the Drovers' Inn, its weary team of six stout draft horses apparently undisturbed by the shooting. A series of heads and faces showed above the batwing doors of the saloon—daytime boozers and off-duty cowhands gawking at the action. Ben put a bullet in the whitewashed false front of the structure, inches above the batwings, to move the men out of the line of fire.

"I'm going to hustle over to the beer wagon," he said. "That way we'll have them more or less between us."

"Ain't fair," Nick said with a grin. "You'll have a better shot, but I'll be stuck here alone, listenin' to them women carryin' on in the back." A flurry of slugs peppered the doorway and the display area, shattering the glass remaining in the frame of the front window, punching holes in sacks of seed, and flinging ruptured and spewing canned goods from the shelves.

"Might as well get to it," Ben said as he pushed himself to his feet. Nick moved up next to him, drawing his bone-gripped Colt and placing it on the floor just inside the door. He jacked open his shotgun, thumbed a pair of shells into the breach, and snapped the weapon shut.

"Ready when you are, Ben. Watch yourself."

Ben reloaded his rifle. "Yeah," he said. "I will." He felt his muscles tense for a moment, and then he balanced on the balls of his feet like a runner awaiting a starter's gun. He nodded to Nick. No more words were needed.

Nick fired a round from his shotgun and then another, so that the two blasts sounded almost as one. Before the smoking long gun struck the floor, Nick was firing his Colt, not seeking targets but putting as much lead in the air as he could as Ben raced and weaved across Main Street.

Ben fired rapidly, working the lever of the rifle smoothly and quickly as he ran, dancing away from the hail of death seeking him, until the hammer clicked sharply on the empty chamber. He threw the rifle the few remaining yards to the beer wagon, and, too fast for an eye to follow, his twin Smith & Wesson .45s were in his hands, spewing lead at the riflemen on the bank roof. Spouts of dust tagged after him on the street, and a slug buzzed past his ear. To his side and across the street behind him, the chatter of Nick's pistol fire halted and was replaced, once again, by the booming roar of his shotgun. Ben smiled. *Sure wish I could keep him in Burnt Rock. The kid might make a lawman yet—he's loadin' his shotgun with one hand and firing his Colt with the other.*

He dove to safety—for the second time that day—and tucked his head as he rolled to his feet. The beer wagon was a broad-beamed and stalwart freighter, loaded two-high with barrels of beer in lines of three. Ben holstered his handguns, snatched up the 30.30, and vaulted onto the bed of the wagon, then slid cartridges into the breach of his rifle. The aroma of beer filled the air around him; on the bank's side of the wagon, perhaps thirty foaming streams of the liquid arced out from bullet holes in the barrels.

Ben aimed, drew a breath, and eased pressure onto his trigger. The suddenly lifeless hands of an outlaw on the roof unclenched and dropped a Winchester to the street.

A moment later a voice sounded from within the bank. "Marshall! I'm comin' out with a woman in front of me! You or your deputy fire, and I'll kill her!" The front door of the bank swung open, and a man walked out, his arm around a woman's neck and the muzzle of his pistol jammed under her jaw.

Lee's appearance in the doorway struck Ben like a punch to the stomach. The danger to her changed everything.

"Here's what's gonna happen," the outlaw called out. "My boys'll bring our horses 'round, and we'll mount up. This little lady," he said as he forced his pistol barrel more deeply under Lee's chin, eliciting a quick yelp of pain, "is ridin' in front of me, on my horse. You do anything I don' want you to, an' she dies, no questions asked. We'll let her go when we don' need her no more, an' not before. Another thing, Marshall: You got a bank president bleedin' out on the floor in there. Looks like he could use a doc."

"Let her go now, and we won't follow for an hour," Ben shouted from behind his cover. "You got my word on that. Let—"

"I ain't offerin' to deal with you, lawman! You do it my way or the woman dies. An' then we'll wear you an' your deputy down an' kill you like sick dogs an' go through this stinkin' town an' gun everythin' that moves!"

Ben chewed on his lower lip and thought for a moment. Burnt Rock was a West Texas settlement that existed only to serve the cattle trade, and the cavalry had been the primary source of law before he had been hired by the town. Now the army was dealing with hostile Indians, so the sad truth was that the outlaw was right—the sheer firepower of the gang would present a siege that he, Nick, and the few men in town brave enough to handle a gun couldn't possibly withstand—or survive. And the outlaw would make good on his threat to destroy the town and murder its citizens. He'd done it before, in other places. Ben knew the man. He knew more about Zebulon Stone than he cared to.

"Ben," Nick called from the mercantile. "Don't let him—"

"You hush, boy!" Ben snapped. Louder, he called out to the outlaw, "I got no choice, and that's what you're playin' on."

"Stand up where I can see you, with your hands empty—your deputy too."

Ben complied and climbed down from the wagon. As he moved out into the street, he held his palms at chest level in front of him. In a moment, Nick stepped through the pocked and splintered door frame of the mercantile and joined him.

Stone said something over his shoulder that Ben couldn't hear, and two men led a string of saddled horses out of the alley next to the bank. The gunhands on the roof clambered down ladders leaning on either side of the building and mounted, bringing their horses in front of Stone as he hefted Lee into the saddle of a tall chestnut and swung up behind her. Stone held his pistol more loosely now, with the muzzle lightly touching the side of her neck. After one of his men handed him the chestnut's reins, he turned the horse out a few steps into the street and pointed him at Ben.

"You remember me, lawman?"

"I remember."

"Then this ain't over, now is it?"

"Not nearly, Stone. It's not nearly over."

Ben's eyes met Lee's. He saw fear in them, but he also saw the strength he'd seen many times before. The endless depth of the chestnut brown and the minute flecks of gold even now reminded him of a calm pool that violence and hatred could never touch. Her lips, pale and bloodless lines, moved slowly and soundlessly. "Take him, Ben!" they urged. He had to look away from her face. A move against Stone would guarantee her death—and probably Nick's and his own as well. He looked back at Stone.

The outlaw was taking a twisted cheroot from his vest pocket with his free hand and sticking it in the corner of his mouth. He scratched a lucifer on the cantle of his saddle and lit the cigar. From a haze of smoke he said, "That's good, lawman. You jist keep your wits about you." He exhaled a plume of smoke past Lee's face. "I said I was gonna kill you twenty years ago, but you got lucky. That ain't gonna happen this time. An' I'm gonna do it my way—the slow way." He gigged his horse lightly with his spurs and pulled up directly in front of Ben. "You know somethin', Marshall?" he continued. "Your pa died real slow—an' he was yellin' an' screamin' at the end so it like to give me a headache."

Ben's hands twitched slightly, but he held them where they were. He could feel the raw, electric tension between him and Stone, as palpable as the steel point of an arrow at full draw and straining to be released. For a full minute the only sound on the street was that of Lee's constricted breathing.

"Let her go, Stone," Ben finally said, struggling to control his voice. "If you don't, I'll watch you die, and your men too. If you don't know anything else about me, you know I don't threaten anything I can't do. Let her go."

Stone sucked on his cigar strongly enough so that the end of it appeared white hot, even in the direct light of the punishing sun. He expelled tendrils of smoke through his nostrils and then a tight stream through his pursed lips. "I could real easy kill you right where you stand."

"If you thought you could, you would." Ben was relieved to hear that his voice sounded more controlled. "I'm faster than you've ever been, an' a whole lot more accurate. I think I've proved that. If it wasn't for the lady you're hiding behind, you'd be on your back in the street with flies walking on your eyes."

Redness suffused Stone's neck and engulfed his face. His eyes became glinting black diamonds. He spat his cigar off to one side. "You're nothin' without your voodoo book, Flood, an' I'm gonna prove that real soon."

"My Bible? You're right—I'm not. But that doesn't change anything. You're going down hard and you're going down to stay the next time we meet."

Stone didn't reply, but instead spun his horse and loped back to the bank. His men let him pass and then followed him, leaving their dead comrades where they'd fallen.

In a moment Nick was at Ben's side. "C'mon! You heard what he said about Mr. Turner! He needs . . . Ben? What's the matter?"

Ben shook his head, feeling like a man just coming awake. He saw Nick staring at him. "C'mon," he grunted and set out at a run to the bank.

He found Sam Turner on his back, semiconscious with blood pooling beneath him and onto the polished wooden floor. Marcia Hildebrand, one of the tellers, knelt at his side. Face ashen and fingers trembling, she wiped oily sweat from his forehead with her handkerchief.

Ben eased Marcia back by her shoulders and took her position next to Sam. His fingers gently probed the two wounds. "Get Doc," he said to Nick. "An' get him fast. Sam's bleeding awful bad. Marcia—I need some long strips of cloth." He looked over at Hiram standing dumbstruck against the wall, his hands hanging like useless appendages at his side.

"Hiram!"

It took a moment for the man to respond. When he did, his voice cracked with emotion. "I . . . opened the safe. He made me do it. He shot Mr. Turner without a word, and he took Miss Morgan with him—"

"There's no time to talk, Hiram. I need you to run over to the Drovers' and get a quart of the cheapest, rawest rotgut there is."

"I . . . shouldn't have opened—"

"Do like I said, and do it now!" Ben shouted. "Marcia—where's that cloth?"

Sam's eyes opened at the sound of Ben's voice. "Lord," he whispered.

"He's here, Sam. You know that." He took his friend's hand in his own.

"It hurts . . ."

"Yeah, I know it hurts. Just hold on, all right?"

Sam's eyes closed. His lips moved slightly, producing the most silent of whispers. Then his lips were still.

"Marcia!"

Ben looked over his shoulder and saw Marcia scurrying over to him with cloth in her hands. He took two strips, wound them together, and fit them around the upper aspect of Sam's right leg. When he jerked the knot tight, Sam grunted and then lapsed back into unconsciousness. The blood stopped flowing almost immediately.

The shoulder wound, however, was not so easy. Blood pumped from the torn flesh in gushes, in time with the banker's heart. Ben's index finger found the wound, and he pressed it closed, feeling solid bone underneath.

At that moment, Hiram burst back into the bank and raced across the floor to Ben's side, extending an opened bottle of varnish-hued whiskey. Ben shook his head.

"You pour it—right below the tourniquet, directly into the wound. I can't let go here."

Hiram tipped the neck of the bottle carefully, dripping the whiskey onto Sam's leg.

“Pour it, Hiram!” Ben demanded. “Soak the whole area and then start up here on his shoulder—infection will kill him just as dead as a bullet will.”

As Hiram poured the whiskey, Nick banged through the front door of the bank with a middle-aged man in a rumpled suit right behind him.

“Doc!” Ben exclaimed. “Thank God you’re here.”

The doctor’s craggy face creased with a frown, and he ran his fingers through his long, uncombed mass of black and gray hair. “You did the right things, Ben,” he said, his voice deep and throaty. “Shift on out of the way now and let me in where you are. You can let go of the artery.”

Ben rose to his feet and stood at Sam’s head, watching Doc at work. Nick and Hiram stood by his side.

“You boys go now,” Doc said. “If I need anything, I’ll call for you.”

Obediently, the men filed out of the bank. Ben looked at the undertaker’s wagon baking in the sun as two men hefted the bodies of the dead outlaws into it. He turned to the bank teller.

“Hiram,” he said gently, “you go on home. You’ve had enough excitement for one day.”

Hiram nodded and started shuffling away.

“One thing I want you to know,” Ben said loudly enough for those gathered in the street to hear. “You did the right thing earlier today, and you saved some lives by doing it. Ain’t a whole lot of men who would’ve been able to keep their wits under the guns of those outlaws.”

Hiram hesitated midstep without looking back. Then his spine straightened and his shuffle became a stride.

Ben watched him walk away for a moment and then sat on the bench in front of the bank. Nick sat next to him.

"You gonna tell me how that outlaw knew you?" Nick asked. He quickly added, "I heard just about everything that passed between the two of you from over at Scott's. I couldn't help it. You wasn't but ten or fifteen feet from me."

Ben sighed and looked down at his clenched hands. "Zeb Stone was ridin' with a gang of border raiders twenty years ago. They ran off a few head of my father's cattle, an' he went after them. They killed him. I was workin' for the Pinkerton outfit in Yuma when I got the telegram from my ma. I came back, and I faced Stone, and I put a bullet in his gut and left him to die. He didn't."

Nick was quiet for a long moment. "What's that voodoo thing he talked about?" he finally asked. "I never heard a Bible called a voodoo book. Fact is, I don't know what voodoo is, least not for sure. It's some kind of magic, ain't it?"

"It's pure evil is what it is. Calling Scripture voodoo is about the worst insult I can think of for the Word of God."

The two men sat in silence. The small crowd of townspeople began wandering away from the bank, some to the Drovers' Inn, some to their jobs, some to their homes. Soon only two men remained, engaging in a drunken push-and-shove match near the beer wagon.

"You want me to take care of that?" Nick asked.

"Let it go. Nobody's going to get hurt. Those two chuckleheads are the best of friends. They both ride for the Q-Bar, an' they're off till the next herd moves out. It's the beer talking, not the men."

"Yessir."

Ben watched the two men until they ceased their bickering and walked back to the Drovers' Inn. "You did good today, Nick," he said after a moment. "I'd still rather see you with a rifle than with that shotgun of yours, but I guess that's up to you." He paused. "No sense in dancin' around it—we're both thinkin' about Lee being with Stone and his men."

"Yessir, we are—an' we can't trust that snake's word. He ain't gonna let Miss Morgan go no matter what he said. I'd like to put together a posse and ride out as soon as we can get provisioned. Maybe we—"

"We can't do that—not right now," Ben interrupted. "A bunch of men riding after Stone will guarantee Lee dies. And if we got close enough to fight, the shopkeepers an' farmers we might gather up would die too. Stone's men have at least one Sharp's, an' it'll drop a bull buffalo dead at a mile. A good rifleman'd pick us off one at a time."

Nick stood, his hands forming and releasing fists at his side. "What're we gonna do then?"

"Well, you're gonna be the only law in Burnt Rock for a little while. I'm leavin' you in charge."

"Leavin' me in charge? What're you sayin', Ben? I ain't about to let you ride out alone after them outlaws!"

Ben frowned. "I'm givin' you an order, Nick. I expect it to be obeyed. I'm going to get some gear together and ride after dark. You're stayin' to protect the town. That's the way it's going to be, an' I don't want to hear any argument."

Nick stood in front of Ben and glared down at him. "There's no way you can stop me from goin' with you. You need my gun to take on Stone. The town will keep."

"You heard what I said."

"I don't care what you said! I ain't one to disobey one of your orders—you know that. But this time I will, an' you can count on that."

Ben met Nick's eyes. "Give me your badge."

"What?"

"You heard me. Give me your badge. And remember what I told you when I took you on to train as a deputy: If you take off that badge because of a dispute with me, you never put it on again in my town."

Nick's right hand began to move to the left side of the leather vest he wore over his shirt. His fingers trembled slightly, although they'd been as steady as those of a surgeon during the gunfight. His fingertips touched the badge, and his thumb and forefinger slid behind it to the clasp.

"This ain't fair, and you know it." His voice was tight, as if he had to force each word from his mouth.

"I never said nothin' about any part of this job bein' fair."

Nick's hand hesitated, faltered, and then dropped to his side quickly, as if it had suddenly lost the power required to remove the star and toss it into the dust at Ben's feet.

They stared hard at each other for another moment. Ben couldn't tell which one of them softened first. Probably Nick, whose grin was forced but necessary.

"Seems to me you're awful feisty for an ol' man," he said.

Ben smiled. "Could be you got a good point there," he said. "Let's check on Sam, an' then I gotta saddle up."

The coppery smell of blood and sweat met them as they eased through the door to the bank. "Doc?" Ben asked quietly from across the room. The physician didn't turn from his work. Sam was bare from the waist up, his head elevated a few inches by the bank ledger upon which it rested. Doc had prepared a bandage and sling from Sam's shirt. Another bandage was wrapped around the man's leg. He seemed to be resting peacefully, but his face was bathed in a sheen of sweat.

"I'll need a wagon to move him home in a couple of hours," Doc said. "He's going to make it. I don't know how much good his arm will be, but he'll live."

Ben released a long whoosh of breath he didn't realize he'd been holding. "You need anything here?"

"No. He lost lots of blood. Your tourniquet probably saved his life. And if that didn't, putting pressure on the artery did. Good work."

"I doubt that it was me who saved him. But thanks—and thanks for comin'. Once again, we owe you more than we can ever pay."

Doc nodded as he adjusted the shoulder bandage. Ben watched him tend to Sam for a few more minutes, then turned to walk back outside. Nick followed him.

"I need your help in getting some things together," Ben said outside the bank. "I need ammunition for my Colt and for my 30.30—and I'm wondering if the bandoleers we took off those bandits last month will carry rifle slugs."

"30.30s will fit nice an' tight. I'll load 'em both up. Four canteens?"

"How many do we have?"

"Maybe six or seven," Nick said. "Corks're good on all of them, even the army stuff."

"Good. Fill 'em all. I'll need as much jerky as we can stuff in my saddlebags too. I'll check Snorty's shoes myself, but he should be OK. I had his iron reset just last week. I don't know how much grazing there'll be, so I need to take a feed bag of good oats." He reflected for a moment. "I guess that's pretty much it."

Nick nodded. "I'll start getting things together. I just . . . I wish I was ridin' out with you, is all."

"I know that. But we can't leave the town without a lawman."

Nick nodded his head again, then turned to walk away. Rather than going into his office, Ben walked around to the back of the building, where his horse, Snorty, was picking through a quarter bale of hay in the post-and-rail enclosure Ben had built.

He had his mount saddled and ready when Nick clattered into the enclosure with the canteens and other gear. They loaded Ben's saddlebags and hung three canteens from the saddle horn and three more from the latigo ties behind the cantle.

"Keep your eyes open," Nick said as Ben mounted.

"Yeah. I will. Take care of my town."

Then he rode through the alley next to his office and turned left on Main Street toward the open prairie. He put Snorty into a lope as soon as he passed the last building.

2

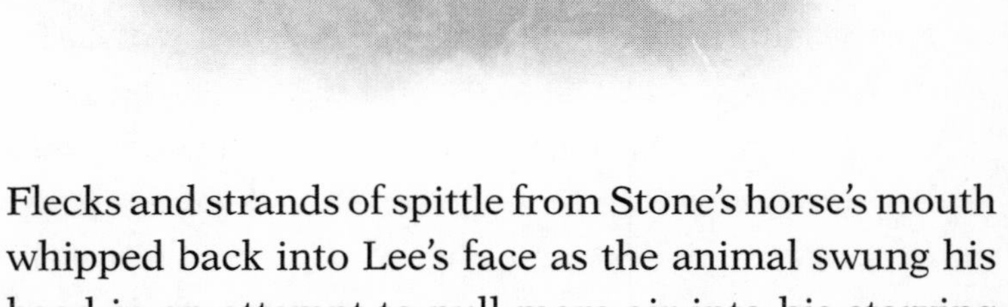

Flecks and strands of spittle from Stone's horse's mouth whipped back into Lee's face as the animal swung his head in an attempt to pull more air into his starving lungs. When the horse stumbled slightly, Stone viciously slashed a length of rein across its neck.

"Can't you see you're killing this poor horse?" Lee demanded. "Let him—let all of these horses—rest!"

She heard Stone, who was riding behind her on the horse's rump, chuckle in response. The next moment, she was airborne, swept from her seat in the saddle. Slamming into the prairie floor, her chin gouged a rut in the sand and grit, and her arms flailed helplessly. The sharp edge of a rock opened a thin, razorlike incision the length of her jawbone.

Outlaws swerved around her, laughing. As she pushed herself to a sitting position, blood cascaded from both nostrils onto her high-collared white blouse. Her slip, petticoat, and ankle-length skirt fluffed around her in the dirt.

Stone hollered to the dozen men behind him and then wrenched his horse into a U-turn and drew rein in front of her. The other gang members followed. Stone took a cigar from his shirt pocket, bit off the end, and spat it next to her. She glared at him, her anger overcoming the fear that had numbed her since they'd ridden out of Burnt Rock two hours before.

"Looks like it's time to set some rules here," Stone said, lighting his cigar. "First thing: You don' tell me nothin' about nothin'. That clear? You do what I say, an' I'll let you live. You don', an' I'll put a bullet right between them pretty brown eyes of yours." He blew thick smoke into the air between them. "On the other hand, could be I won't gun you. I might jist let my boys have at you." He nodded toward the man Lee had kneed at the bank. "Danny here don' take real good to bein' knocked down by a woman. He might want to kinda even up things between you an' him. Am I sayin' the truth, Danny?"

The man was hunched forward slightly in his saddle, and his face glistened with a sheen of pain-generated sweat. "Ain't nothin' I'd like better, Boss," he growled.

Stone laughed. "Least your voice ain't changed too much. If it gits any higher, though, I gotta git rid of you. I don' want no geldings ridin' with me."

The other outlaws laughed loudly, and Danny's face went from the pale hue of pain to the crimson shade of embarrassment. "I'll give you my share of what we got from the bank, Boss. Lemme have 'er—sell 'er to me."

Stone ignored the man. "See what I mean?" he said to Lee. "Ain't nothin' you can do about—"

"There's a lot Ben Flood can do about this—and he will," Lee said. She was pleased to hear that her voice sounded angry rather than frightened.

Stone's eyes remained fixed on her as she swept her hand across the front of her face, wiping away blood from her nose. His mouth began to turn up in a mocking grin, but stopped.

"What's between you an' Flood?"

"We're friends. He takes friendship seriously, and so do I."

Now the grin was completed. "Friends? Aww, that's real nice. Does that friendship include him parkin' his boots under your bed, little lady? Don' his voodoo book say somethin' against that?"

Lee's cheeks reddened. She started to speak but then closed her mouth. Stone's pistol was in his hand faster than she could follow, and suddenly she was deaf and almost blind from the blast of the weapon. For a moment she saw nothing but colors merging together and drifting in front of her, and she could no longer hear the labored breathing of the horses. She swallowed hard. When she spoke, her voice sounded as if she were speaking at the bottom of a well.

"The horses," she said. "They're—"

"You don' know nothin' 'bout horses," Stone answered. "Ain't nothin' wrong with this ol' boy 'cept he's gittin' lazy."

Lee swallowed again, and her ears cleared a bit. "All I'm saying is that these animals need water badly. Some of them are already weaving, and a couple are beyond the point where they can sweat anymore—they'll die without water."

"Woooo-eee!" Stone mocked. "You ain't nothin' but an ol' wrangler!" Around him, the other outlaws chuckled. "Ridin' a church pew with your voodoo man's 'bout all the ridin' you do, little lady."

She met the outlaw's eyes but didn't answer.

"You Flood's church partner, sweet thing?" he went on. "You an' him set right up in front of a Sunday mornin'?"

He dismounted as Lee struggled to her feet, her hands sweeping ineffectually at the dirt on her skirt. In a couple of strides, he was in front of her. When he raised his hand, she didn't cringe. He held his pose for a moment, then delivered the blow, his palm striking her cheek with a sound like the crack of a bullwhip. She stumbled back a step, but her eyes never left his face.

"Git on the horse," Stone said. "An' keep your yap shut until I talk to you. That there was jist a taste of what you'll git if you cause me any trouble. Only reason you ain't dead right now is that I need you to make sure Flood's after me. Soon's he's done, so are you. The only thing is how you die—whether I gun you quick or I give you to Danny an' the boys." He leered at her then turned to the gang. "Mount up!"

Lee refused to allow Stone the pleasure of watching her raise a hand to the cheek that felt as if lamp oil had been poured on it and then lighted. Instead, she moved to where Stone's horse stood, sweat dripping from his chest and belly, and stroked his muzzle gently.

The animal flinched when she moved her hand toward his face, but he calmed immediately when he felt her touch. After a moment she stepped to the horse's side. She swung into the saddle effortlessly, her high-buttoned shoes a foot above the stirrups. Her left hand touched the horn of Stone's saddle, and her right rested in her lap.

Stone mounted behind her wordlessly, settling himself onto the horse's rump, reaching around Lee with his left hand to hold the reins. He banged his spurs against the horse's sides, and the weary animal lumbered into a semblance of a lope.

The outlaws gave their boss the lead and spread out a bit in a ragged arrowhead, as if trying to avoid eating the dust of the point rider. One man stuck close to Stone, riding back a few yards on Lee's right side. Every so often the man nudged his horse into a faster gait and drew up almost parallel to her. She met Danny's eyes and refused to look away, but a shiver that contradicted the heat climbed up her spine each time he pulled closer.

She had been around hard and desperate men enough times to recognize that she had shamed the outlaw. She had taken away from him the only thing that mattered in his life: his reputation. The laughs of Stone and the others had cut him more deeply than any knife could. After all, a knife could only kill him; what she had done was worse than death. She had humbled him, dropped him to the floor like a kicked puppy. She knew that in his mind, she deserved to die.

After a while, the dull, mindless monotony of the ride ground away the sharpest edges of Lee's fear. A tiny ember of anger that had begun to grow when Stone had slapped her was increasing in size in her mind and heart. She nurtured the sensation. *Better to be mad than scared,* she thought. *There's a way out of this. There has to be.* She straightened her back a bit, sitting taller in the saddle.

Stone reined in, dropping his horse to an exhausted, toe-dragging walk. Many of the mounts of the gang were equally weary.

"We'll set up by them trees ahead," he said. "There's water an' some grazing for the horses." He looked out at his gang. "Danny—you an' Luke go on out an' drop us some grub. I ain't about to eat jerky after a score like we made today."

Danny edged his horse closer to Stone and Lee. "What're you gonna do with her?" he asked. "I don' mind doin' some huntin', but I need to know what you're gonna do with this woman. And I ain't ridin' out till I know."

Stone shifted his horse so that he was sideways to Danny. "Oh? You sayin' I don' know how to keep a prisoner, Dan? Is that what you're sayin'? You thinkin' Miss Pretty here's gonna escape before you git back?"

"That ain't it, Zeb, an' you know it. Thing is, she's *mine*."

Stone slid down from his horse and took a few steps toward Danny. Stopping and widening his stance slightly, he placed his left foot several inches ahead of his right.

His gun hand hung next to the pearl grips of his revolver. A wash of sweat broke across Danny's forehead.

"You . . . you got no call to draw on me, Boss. All I was sayin' was—"

"What you was sayin' is it's you who gives the orders in this gang, an' it's you who makes the decisions. That's what you was sayin'."

Danny's throat moved, as if he were swallowing a lump. Taking a hesitant step backward, he focused his eyes on Stone's gun hand. He looked as if he knew he was going to die. But it appeared that he *had* to draw—it was better than being shot down with his weapon still holstered. Sweat dripped into his eyes, and he squinted against the sting.

"Mr. Stone," Lee snapped, her voice as strident as that of a schoolmarm addressing a classroom of unruly youngsters, "I've been riding for several hours without stopping, and now I need some privacy. I'll walk ahead to the trees. I'll expect you and your men to wait here."

Stone burst out laughing, as did most of his men. Danny swallowed hard once again and then forced a laugh that squeaked as it left him.

"If that don't beat a full house, I dunno what does," Stone sputtered. "First, it's my friend Danny here takin' over my gang, an' now I got a woman givin' me orders 'bout when she wants to tinkle!" He turned to his men. "I s'pose I oughta jist up an' retire from outlawin'—git me a job as a store clerk or a preacher!"

The gang stood gaping at their boss. For a moment there was an uneasy silence. Lee couldn't help but wonder what they all must be thinking. Their boss's bursts of joviality were probably just as likely to lead to bloodshed as to laughter.

Stone looked away from his gang and nodded to Lee. "Go on, then—I'll give you a couple of minutes an' no longer."

Lee strode off toward the copse fifty yards ahead of her with the uncomfortable knowledge that the eyes of Zeb Stone's murderous gang were on her back. She forced herself to walk normally, but she felt tightness across her shoulders and queasiness in her stomach. She knew she'd saved a man's life a few moments ago, but that thought gave her little consolation. *He'll still be happy to kill me as soon as Stone gives him permission to do so.*

She pushed the thought of Danny away and remembered the blaze she'd seen in Ben's eyes as he'd attempted to negotiate her release. She'd never seen that fire before in all the two years they'd known each other.

She almost felt like smiling as she thought of how they'd first met. Within a week after she'd bought and moved onto the Wesson farm, Ben had ridden up to introduce himself. She'd noticed his manners—she always noticed good manners in men—and had found him far more gentle and introspective than she'd thought a Texas lawman could be. She'd made tea, and she'd had a difficult time keeping a straight face as his callused fingers attempted to handle the delicate china tea set she'd inherited from her mother.

She'd also been surprised to find that Ben was a Christian. The fact that he was a gunslinger—a man who killed when necessary—disturbed her. But over the past couple of years, her feelings toward Ben had strengthened and grown, and she knew he felt the same about her.

Lee's thoughts were suddenly jerked away from Ben. The chunk of shod hooves on the dirt told her horses were approaching, but she didn't turn to the sound. Zeb Stone rode up to her and slowed his horse to her pace.

"You said you'd give me some privacy."

"Yeah. I don' want you wanderin' off, though. Fact is, if you try anything, I'm gonna have Danny come after you. I'm gonna tell him I don' want you back, jist that I want him to find you. See what I mean?"

Lee took a deep breath before speaking. She wanted her voice to show no emotion. "I have no choice but to obey your orders at this point. But this isn't going to last long, and then you'll pay for what you've done."

"Your beau gonna gun me?" Stone said with a smirk. "That ain't the way it's gonna be. What you are right now is bait, sweet thing, whether you know it or not. I spent a lot of time settin' this whole thing up, an' I'm gonna meet Ben Flood jist like I did once before—in a saloon, in front of lots of witnesses. Only difference is, this time I'm gonna kill him, an' I'm gonna watch him die."

The frigidity in the outlaw's voice made Lee shudder, yet she couldn't bite back her response born of the fear, frustration, and humiliation she'd suffered at the outlaw's hands. "You're not half the man Ben Flood is!"

Stone leaned to the side and grasped for Lee's hair, a curse forming on his lips. Lee stumbled away from the hand clawing at her and instinctively raised her own hands to her face—and then she saw the opportunity she'd waited for all day. Stone was leaning far out of his saddle, off balance.

She saw an image of it in her mind. Grasping Stone's arm at the elbow, she could shift her body at the waist and use Stone's momentum and her own strength to wrench him off the horse and onto the ground. She'd scream at Stone's horse and swing into the saddle with a running mount and . . . then what? The weary horse didn't have enough pluck in him to move faster than a lope, and a few of the men in the gang were riding good stock, horses she could see had bottom and heart. *Would Stone make good on his promise to send Danny after me? Would he come himself?* Either way, she knew she'd be recaptured and killed—or raped first and then killed.

Lee turned her back just as Stone tackled her from his saddle, taking them both down in a heap of boots and skirts and dirt. Her breath was knocked from her as she struck the prairie, and she heard a quiet "pop" inside her head as her nostrils once again began to pump blood. Stunned but able to move, she tucked herself as tightly as she could, arms over her face, awaiting the fists and boots she knew would come. The ground shook under her as the gang rode up, and she gagged on the salty blood that ran into her mouth.

But the blows didn't come. The world became as silent as the inside of a casket. Nothing moved. It was as if even time had ceased to pass, as if the universe was waiting with her for that first jolt of pain. Lee held her eyes closed so tightly that red shapes floated inside her eyelids. *Please, Lord . . .*

"Git up."

She wasn't sure of what she'd heard. She didn't move for a moment. Then she opened her eyes and slowly brought herself to a sitting position. When her feet were under her, she stood. The evil—the frenzied glisten in Stone's eyes—forced a gasp from her.

The outlaw's voice trembled, and his words seemed clipped, as if each of them had to be forced past the tight white lines of his lips. "The next time you mouth off to me, you'd better have a gun on me an' be ready to kill me, 'cause there's no other way you'll live another minute."

Lee's voice was as calm as she could make it. "I still need a moment of privacy."

"Go then." Stone faced his men. "I changed my mind. We ain't stoppin' till mornin'. We'll water the horses an' rest 'em an hour, then we're ridin' out." He faced Danny and Luke. "Like I already said, I want you boys to go on ahead an' kill somethin' for us to eat in the mornin'. Wash it up good an' hang it so it don't rot overnight."

Luke nodded, gathering his reins. Danny began to speak but then clamped his mouth shut. He wheeled his horse, and the two men rode off.

When Lee returned to the waiting outlaws, she carried in her pocket a narrow, three-inch-long piece of stone, probably shale or flint, that she'd noticed near the base of a much larger rock. The edge of the piece wasn't sharp—she ran her thumb over it without a cut—but the tip was triangular and could be considered a primative stabbing weapon. She'd smiled ruefully when she dropped the piece of stone into the pocket of her skirt; it was better than no weapon at all, but not by much. Still, the slight weight of it was comforting. She was no longer unarmed.

"This plug can't carry double no more," Stone announced as Lee walked up to him. "You're gonna ride on that chestnut over there." He pointed to a lean, hard-faced man slouching in the saddle of a horse that appeared to be an unlikely crossing of a Thoroughbred and a Clydesdale. The horse's chest was broad, and his ears indicated alertness. Lee noticed immediately that his legs were straight, and his coat showed he'd gotten more care than most of the other outlaws' mounts. This one, Lee decided, wouldn't give a good short horse a race, but he could probably cover ground forever.

She walked to the hawk-faced man. As she stood looking up at him, she guessed that, although he was Mexican, there was Indian blood in his very near ancestry. But what most drew her eyes to his face was a raised scar that ran from his right ear downward, through both lips, and under his jaw. On first glance, the scar looked fresh because of its swollen redness, but she noticed that the flesh appeared hard and settled, as if it had been there for a long time.

Her gaze traveled to the horse again. The bit in the chestnut's mouth was what Mexicans called a *spada,* and it had long, curving shanks. Inside the horse's mouth was a frog, a silver plate the size of a twenty-dollar gold piece that crushed the animal's tongue against the floor of its mouth and put sharp pressure on the bars, the sensitive areas behind the horse's teeth along the jawline.

"This bit is cruel," she said. "It looks like you take some care of your horse—why not get that thing out of his mouth and—"

"I ride him, he carries me, we have no arguments." The man slid his left foot out of the stirrup. "Stone says you ride with me, then you ride with me. Get up behind me or argue it out with him. I don' care."

Lee slid her foot into the stirrup and eased onto the horse's rump. It took less than a minute for the stench of the body in front of her to cause her to begin breathing through her mouth. The outlaw was redolent with the smell of wine, unwashed clothing, and old sweat.

Stone had mounted as well and was talking with a Mexican outlaw. The man, gaunt almost to the point of emaciation, had a yellowish-looking cigarette drooping from the corner of his mouth. He drew on it frequently, making the ember glow, but didn't take it from his mouth.

Lee could make out only a few words of their conversation. ". . . bring him to me—don' kill him . . . five thousand dollars plus your share of the bank . . ."

Lee tensed, and her fingers grasped the cantle tightly. They were talking about Ben. She shuddered as fear crept up her spine. If Ben were captured, both their lives were over.

3

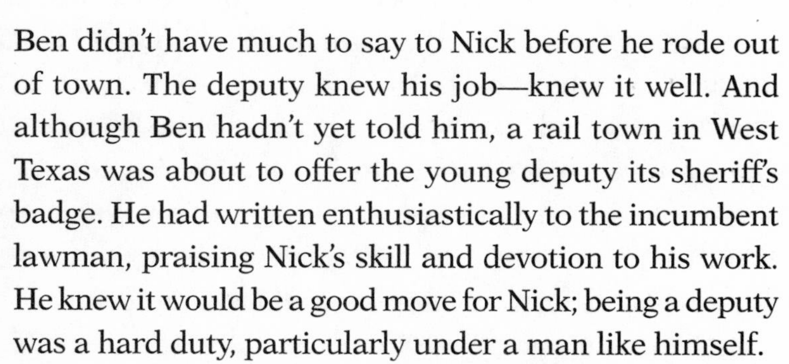

Ben didn't have much to say to Nick before he rode out of town. The deputy knew his job—knew it well. And although Ben hadn't yet told him, a rail town in West Texas was about to offer the young deputy its sheriff's badge. He had written enthusiastically to the incumbent lawman, praising Nick's skill and devotion to his work. He knew it would be a good move for Nick; being a deputy was a hard duty, particularly under a man like himself.

The moon that night was half full, affording plenty of light for riding. Ben didn't bother to search for tracks; he knew Stone was headed either for Mexico or a hide-out in the same direction. With the robbery so fresh, the outlaws wouldn't head to a major city, where there'd be both lawmen and bounty hunters.

Snorty had been a tad fractious as they left Burnt Rock, doing some crow-hopping and even pitching strongly a couple of times. He wanted to run, and he was showing his frustration in every way he could, outside of flat-out fighting to get his head. Once they got to the outskirts of town, Ben gave Snorty all the loose rein he wanted, and the horse launched into a churning scramble of acceleration that lasted only a few strides before he was in a full gallop.

Ben loved the speed as much as Snorty did. The cool, liquid rush of night air that still tasted faintly of the sun, the steady, pounding *thunk* of hooves as they struck the sand, the sharp glint of the moon and uncountable stars, all brought Ben as close to God as he felt he could be in this life. But tonight there was a deadly urgency to his speed, and it drained his pleasure. Tonight, the moon and stars were simply sources of light to help him find Lee.

After a couple of fast miles, Ben brought Snorty down to an easy, ground-covering lope. Snorty, true to his name, woofed through his nostrils in satisfaction, his edge of nervousness gone. Then Ben rode in a fashion introduced to him by an Indian friend: galloping for four or five minutes, loping for ten, jogging for ten, walking for ten. A horse with the stamina of Snorty could repeat the cycle longer than a good rider could stay awake in the saddle.

This rhythm was an automatic thing, like breathing or blinking his eyes. Although he carried no watch, his internal perception of time told him when the pace needed to be adjusted. There was no thought process involved; he simply knew when a change would be good for Snorty. He rode without effort, more comfortable on his horse's back than in the easy chair he'd ordered from the Sears and Roebuck catalog.

Ben tried to keep his mind clear as he rode, but suddenly an image of his mother's eyes jolted him back almost twenty years. He could see the terror in them and the lines of weariness on her face. He could see the living room of his parents' house; it'd been cold that night, but there was no fire in the fireplace. He could hear his mother's voice . . .

"An' then they come in as brazen as could be an' took your pa's bulls, Benjamin. You know how he felt about them animals. That Zeb Stone, he rode right on up to the porch where I was standin', an' stopped an' had this smirk on his face. He said, 'Thanks for the beef, 'ol woman,' an' I told him them was your pa's prize bulls an' couldn't he take some other cattle. He pulled his gun an' put a bullet right in the bigger bull's eye, an' the poor critter fell right there an' never moved again. I ain't ever gonna forget that smirk, Benjamin. It looked like Satan himself was settin' there on that horse. I had the shotgun we keep around the house right there, behind the door, an' maybe I should have defended our stock, but I was so awful scared that my hands was dancin' and I could hardly think straight. When your pa got home the next day, I couldn't do nothin' to keep him from going after Stone an' his men. I begged him, but you know how he was. He wouldn't listen . . ."

Ben's right hand jerked, startling both his horse and himself. He patted Snorty on the neck with his left hand.

He didn't want to remember facing Zeb Stone in a bar in Juarez. He wished he could burn the memory of that day from his mind with the same finality that a fire had burned the stinking, blood-soaked den of sin to the ground ten days later. He didn't want to remember putting a slug purposely and with forethought in Stone's gut, knowing the outlaw would die an excruciating death. That was the one time in the course of his career in law enforcement that he couldn't justify his actions.

As a rule, he wholeheartedly believed in upholding the law and arresting those who broke it, just as he believed he was performing the life mission God had established for him. His bloody vengeance on Zebulon Stone rode heavily in his mind and in his heart. He'd gone not as a lawman to Juarez, but as a gunfighter, seeking to pay a personal debt with a bullet.

But this is different. This isn't the same as it was twenty years ago. Lee is with killers. This is my job.

After a while, Snorty needed a break from the monotony, and so did Ben. He reined in near a small water hole that reflected the light of the moon on its still surface. He released the cinch of his saddle and allowed the cool night air to circulate under the seat. A quick sweep of his palm under the saddle told him there were no lumps or folds in the blanket, and he eased the saddle back into place on Snorty's withers. After letting his horse drink several long swallows, he had him graze in the scrub grass. Then he ate a handful of jerky and quenched his thirst with the brackish-tasting water, opposite from where his horse had drunk.

After fifteen minutes of rest, they were back on the trail again. Snorty ate miles effortlessly, the smooth motion of his back lulling Ben into a mild state of semi-sleep. When the darkness began to yield to the first subtle light of dawn, Ben searched for some shade in which to spend the day.

But he could not keep his mind from nagging at him like a persistent toothache. He knew that the longer Lee was a captive, the more likely she was to be harmed or killed. Thoughts of what might be happening at Stone's camp brought bile to the back of his throat, and he seethed with an impotent rage. He'd done his best to keep such thoughts locked away, but the cruel images appeared nevertheless.

He knew that a daylight attack on the outlaws would get him killed and, no doubt, forfeit Lee's life as well, but what he knew didn't have much effect on what he felt. There was only one thing he could do at that moment. As he lowered his head in silent prayer, his mind became more clear and focused. He was willing to settle for that.

And he couldn't help but feel some measure of peace as the sunrise made the prairie come alive; the first soft light made the Busted Back range of steep, rugged hills seem as if they were sculpted from gold, while the scattered desert pines slowly became visible as the light gained strength.

A few miles ahead, eight or ten turkey vultures swept in wide circles above the ground. The circles they scribed in the sky became smaller in diameter and came closer to the earth as Ben's eyes followed them. *It could be anything—a dead steer that wandered off from a herd, an old buffalo pulled down by coyotes, a mustang with a broken leg that died of thirst.*

Snorty threw himself ahead as Ben's heels banged his sides. The horse stretched to a gallop in a very few strides. Not until he'd covered almost two miles did Ben slow him to a lope.

He noticed that several of the birds had disappeared from sight, angling in toward their prey. Other vultures were arriving, rapidly growing from mere dots in the morning sky to the squawking, ravenous outcasts that they were. Their raucous, blood-chilling screeches reached him before he'd covered half the distance to where they were landing. He slid his 30.30 from the scabbard at his right knee and levered a cartridge into the chamber. The rifle didn't have the range he needed, but the reverberation of the reports would carry.

He jammed the rifle back into the scabbard and snarled like an enraged animal. *Of course the sound will carry—maybe to the outlaws' camp so Stone can be ready with his Sharp's on a tripod to pick me off. I can't take that chance.*

He held Snorty to a fast lope and covered the last mile at that pace. When he topped a slight rise, he saw about fifteen vultures gathered around a thick patch of scrub and bush. Part of a leg and an entire foot stuck out from the scrub. He got a quick look at it as the vultures shoved and fought for position. The foot was a dull, lifeless white, and it looked small to Ben—his mind told him it was feminine.

He pointed Snorty at the birds and let him run. The vulture farthest from the corpse screamed as the horse's hooves slammed into him, crushing his ribs and wings. Those around the body in the scrub lumbered away from the horse and rider hurtling toward them, their wings flailing in the air as they sought escape.

When he slowed Snorty to a stop, Ben stepped down and walked toward the brush. The air was heavy with the stench of blood and death. He felt as if his boots weighed a thousand pounds as he approached the site of the vulture's malignant feast.

The eyeless corpse of a man gaped up at Ben, its face and body crusted with blood. The body had been stripped of anything useful, including his boots and most of his clothing. Ben had no idea what had led to the man's death, but the gaping hole in his chest told that his end had been quick. He buried the corpse as well as he could, digging the hard ground with his sheath knife and his hands.

Ben did his best to sweep thoughts of Zeb Stone out of his mind as he mounted and pointed Snorty at a small grouping of sparse trees. He dismounted there and pulled his tack from Snorty. Then he rubbed the horse's back and chest with handfuls of dry grass and let him drink from the tepid water in the small sinkhole that fed the trees and the grass around it. Ben too drank from the sinkhole. He couldn't afford to waste canteen water.

The spotty shade of the trees was a blessed relief from the malevolence of the midday sun. Ben walked beyond the sinkhole far enough to be sure of the direction in which the Stone gang was headed and then returned to the shade and slept for six hours.

It was Snorty's woofing and snuffling that finally pulled him out of his sleep. He rolled wildly to one side and came to his knees with his Colt extended in front of him—his mission had returned with the force of an ice-cold bucket of water in the face.

He ate a few pieces of jerky, wishing for a cup of coffee, and then tended to Snorty, rationing some crimped oats and allowing two hats full of water. He grinned. A good Stetson had many more uses than covering a head.

By the time he mounted up, the sun was sliding away. But that made little difference to him. He wouldn't have to search the ground. He could tell from the tracks he'd seen that Stone was headed to the Busted Backs.

The moon had waned a bit since the night before, but the light was still good. The prairie looked like a well-tended pasture in the softness of the night, but appearances were deceiving. The clefts and rocks and ruts were cloaked in the uniform darkness of the prairie, and it took a good horse to pick them out. But Ben had few worries on that account. He knew that Snorty would take him where he needed to go.

Ben was holding Snorty at a walk when the first chain of lightning ignited the sky. The horse's back tightened and his neck became hard, as if he were anticipating a blow. Ben knew that only Snorty's loyalty kept him contained; his instincts screamed at him to run, to get away from what was suddenly tearing apart the sky and bellowing at him from all directions.

The sky changed rapidly as the lightning struck; the weak light of the waning moon became the heavy darkness of a closed coffin. The wind pounded at Ben and Snorty, changing its direction so rapidly that its full force was impossible to avoid. There was no putting a back to this wind—it slapped them with stinging stalks of buffalo grass and peppered them with grit and dirt.

Snorty whirled in an attempt to escape the onslaught, but there was no escape. Ben could feel the horse's panic. He drew Snorty's head to the left as far as he could and took two wraps around the saddle horn with the rest of the rein.

When the rain hit, it was powerful—and cold. Snorty squealed and wouldn't move beyond stilted half steps sideways. Ben talked to the horse, stroked his neck, and very slowly let the rein slip around the horn.

The storm careened away almost as suddenly as it had arrived, leaving behind a sea of mud, thick cloud cover impermeable to the moon, and a brisk wind that dropped the temperature at least fifteen degrees in a matter of minutes.

As he slid out of the saddle, Ben debated on whether or not to build a fire. Then he shook his head at his own foolishness—there probably wasn't a dry piece of anything within ten miles, let alone kindling or firewood, or even mesquite. And even if he had fuel, he couldn't risk a fire. He trudged on beside his horse, taunted by an image of a hot mug of very black and thickly sugared coffee.

Much of the dark sky seemed to follow the storm as it fled. Soon moonlight made travel possible again. Ben checked his horse's cinch, let him drink from a rain-filled depression, and ate a few sticks of jerky. Then he mounted up and began riding.

Snorty had recovered from the effects of the storm, but he was tired, so Ben reduced the lope sequence by half and dropped the gallop because of the treacherous footing the storm had left behind. Toward dawn they came upon a water hole surrounded by a few trees. Ben reined in. He was bone tired and his stomach was growling for food other than salty, wooden-tasting strips of beef.

He used the bandana wrapped around his hand to rub down Snorty's back and chest and then fed him a ration of crimped oats. He hung the saddle blanket over a branch to dry—as well as his denim pants, work shirt, and vest. Then he stretched out on some grass and slept soundly for almost seven hours.

When he woke up, his pants, shirt, and vest were dry and warm from the sun and smelled of the sweet prairie breeze. He dressed and argued his feet into his boots. Then he sat in the sun, wiping down the action of his pistol and his rifle with oil from a small tin can.

The sky was cloudless, and the depth of its blue approached the cyan gleam of a precious stone. An eagle scribed lazy circles above the foothills, seeking prey. Ben fed Snorty from the diminishing supply of oats and forced down several sticks of jerky. And as he checked his gear in preparation for the night's ride, he prayed.

Lord Jesus—I'm not thinkin' like a lawman. I want to tell you that I'm not after revenge for Pa and for Lee—and I can't do that just now. I ask that you help me so that I can *say that to you. An' I ask that you keep Lee safe and help me bring in Stone and his men as I'm sworn to.*

The ground dried during the course of the day, making the storm only a memory. Still, the traveling was more difficult. The closer they drew to the hills, the more uneven the ground became. Snorty wanted to run, but Ben held him to a slow lope, even while the light remained good. But as the sun eased down behind the hills, he slowed his horse to a jog and held him at that gait. Clouds moved in with the darkness, and the slice of moon was stingy with its light. Shadows seemed to blend together into indistinct masses.

Ben stopped after midnight to spend a few minutes out of the saddle while Snorty drank from a depression that still held a couple inches of rainwater. He allowed himself several short swallows of water as well and then stepped into a stirrup. As he sat back in the saddle, he was startled by the shrill cry of a night bird that sounded eerily like a woman screaming. He'd done his best to block the thoughts that prodded him. But now, vile scenes of what could be happening to Lee broke through the wall and formed in the darkness in front of him.

For the first time since the war, he was truly afraid. His hands trembled, and he felt sweat sliding down his sides from his armpits. His heart rattled in his chest, its beat like that of a Gatling gun. His good sense told him he was doing the right thing, traveling at the right pace. But everything else screamed to send Snorty into a headlong gallop.

He used a prayer to chase the demons from his mind and to still his heart. After a couple of miles he sighed heavily and held his right hand in front of his face. It was steady. The Lee Morgan in his mind was smiling, and her warmth encompassed him. He rode on.

Ben jerked awake. He'd been dozing, letting his mount do all the work. Now alert, he looked around. The darkness was as thick as molasses, but some shapes appeared less black than the area surrounding them.

One of those shapes spoke.

"Keep your hands away from them guns, or you're dead right now, lawman." The whiskey-rough voice was followed by a sound no lawman could fail to recognize: the metallic slide and click of a round being levered into place. "Get down offa that horse an' keep your hands high."

"I think you're makin' a big mistake, partner. I ain't no law—"

The slug whistled past Ben's ear a heartbeat before the sharp report reached him. He raised both hands over his shoulders, swung his leg over the saddle, and slid to the ground. Thoughts chased one another through his mind, most of them bitter and self-berating. How many times had he nagged Nick about the life-and-death importance of vigilance? And now he'd been caught asleep in the saddle like a Pinkerton recruit on his first field assignment.

"Step on away from your horse." There was no fear in the voice, and no nervousness either.

The man remained only an indistinct form in Ben's vision, yet he seemed to see Ben much more clearly. Then a vagrant night breeze carried a cloying, musty odor in the air. Ben could smell *hempa,* a wild-growing drug that not only produced a state of mild euphoria but also dilated the pupils of the user's eyes, making night vision significantly more acute.

"I ain't tellin' you again, Flood. I got no reason not to pull this trigger."

Ben felt his heart sink. He had hoped the outlaw was a drifter with no allegiance to Stone. The fact that the man knew his name stepped on that thought.

Ben took a pair of tentative steps away from Snorty, a plan coming together in his mind as he did so. He'd learned a few things about *hempa* from his confrontations with the Mexican vaqueros and American cowboys who smoked the weed. It slowed them down both physically and mentally, making a gunfighter with notches on the grip of his pistol seem clumsy and unsure of his moves. That fact, taken with the alcohol he smelled on the man's breath, might offer the slight edge he needed. The outlaw didn't have to draw—he had a cocked and ready rifle trained on Ben, a rifle that could drop an elk at two hundred yards with a single round. Still, Ben reasoned, any break was better than no break at all.

"Look," he said, "I don't know what this is all about. The Circle D is movin' a herd in a couple of days, and I'm their point man. I can show you the letter from Mr.

Terhune, the man who hired me . . ." As his right hand began to move downward, the sandy soil between his boots exploded, peppering his legs with dirt and pebbles. The outlaw worked the lever as quickly as a man could snap his fingers and at the same time raised the barrel once again to hold its mark on Ben's chest.

"Zeb tol' me you was a tricky one, lawman. He also tol' me he wanted you alive, but if you give me trouble, I'll kill you right here an' it won't make no nevermind. Play it the way you want. Die here or die when I get you in front of Stone. It's up to you."

The outlaw's gravelly voice hadn't changed after the shot. That he was used to fast action was clear.

"Maybe you an' me, we can work something out," Ben said. "I'm carrying money for Mr. Terhune—his shipping fee and payroll. I ain't about to die for it. You get the money, an' we ride in different directions, an' nobody gets hurt."

The gunman's chuckle sounded rich and warm, but his words shattered that impression. "You take me for a idjit, Flood?" He spit toward Ben's feet. "I seen enough of you in that town of yours to know who I'm talkin' to. I don' want to hear nothin' else from you—not a word."

A sliver of moonlight slipped from behind the overcast sky. Ben's captor was a bearded, stocky man with a pair of holstered army Colts low on his hips, tied down with latigo. A single bandoleer crossed his chest, the brass of 30.06 cartridges catching and reflecting the feeble light for a quick moment. Holding his rifle steady, he pointed the bore at Ben's chest. His eyes burned with the effects of the *hempa.*

Ben's arms were becoming tired, and a tingling sensation was creeping its way into his hands. He knew that if he was forced to maintain his position much longer, his arms would become wooden and his hands would be those of an arthritic old man. He wouldn't be able to draw, aim, or fire his pistols with the speed and skill he'd developed over the years. What he needed, he knew, was a distraction—something to cause the outlaw to shift his eyes for the briefest part of a second. And Ben needed that distraction very soon, while his hands could still respond to his commands.

"You're gonna turn your back to me," the outlaw said, "and then you're gonna bring them hands down behind you, an' bring 'em together to be tied. An' I'll tell you this: You even *think* of makin' a move for that Colt, an' I'll open a hole in you big enough to run a buffalo through."

Ben's mind raced, half-formed thoughts tripping over one another. He knew bringing his arms down would put his hand close to his side arm, but he also knew the outlaw would shoot if his hand flinched toward the pistol. He began lowering his arms, slowly drawing his fingers inward toward his palms. He moved his fingers, and the tingling dwindled as he slowly lowered his arms. It was a fool's move, he realized, but he had no choice. His hands were at shoulder height, his right fingers now loose and ready to find the grips they'd become so used to over countless hours of practice. Sweat burned in his eyes, and his throat felt dry and dusty. He shifted some of his weight to his left side, planning to dive in that direction . . .

And it was then that his horse lived up to his name. A sudden, explosive snort cut the silence like the roar of a cannon. The outlaw's eyes instinctively swept in Snorty's direction, and he swung the barrel of his rifle toward the sound at the same time. Ben was already in motion, throwing himself to his left, both hands finding, snagging, and drawing in an adrenaline-fueled motion. The muzzle flash of the outlaw's 30.06 slashed the night at the same time the slug cut a shallow groove over Ben's right ear.

Ben fired twice before his body struck the ground. Rolling and firing again, he came to his knees and shot off two more rounds. There'd been no time to aim, no time to gauge precisely where the outlaw stood. He'd fired at the burst of light—and that was all he needed. The first two rounds staggered the outlaw, shoving him back a step. Then his final two rounds slammed into the man's chest. He was dead before he joined his rifle on the sandy dirt.

Ben stood with stooped shoulders, breathing hard with his Colt in his hand. After a stunned moment, he felt the sweat running like tears from his face. The stink of gunpowder, blood, and his own fear sickened him, and he turned away from where he knew the corpse lay.

He holstered his guns and dragged a shirtsleeve across his face. He moved his lips silently in the darkness.

4

Lee's eyes followed Stone as he rode past her, and a shiver took her for a moment. When the clouds drifted away from the face of the moon, she noticed that the other men were tired, listless, and dull eyed. But Stone sat straight in his saddle, with his eyes constantly in motion and his fingertips within inches of his pistol. The smoke from his stogie burned Lee's eyes and scratched at the inside of her nose. When she sneezed, the big horse under her reacted with a quick side step, and the Mexican outlaw lurched clumsily, fighting for his balance. He cursed his horse as he settled again into the saddle. Stone circled back, grinning.

"Almost lost your seat there, Pablo. You might better stay awake. You go to sleep an' the lady shoves you off your horse, we ain't got nothin' that'd catch her. That'd put an end to you, boy—I'll tell you that for sure." The grin was gone, and his eyes were reptilian in the moonlight.

When the Mexican looked away from his leader, unable to hold eye contact, Stone reined his horse back so that he was side by side with Lee.

"That's jist what you were thinkin', now, wasn't it? Dumpin' the Mex an' ridin' off on that good horse of his?"

Tendrils of cigar smoke drifted toward Lee, and she used her left hand to dissipate them. "Whatever it takes is what I'll do."

She hadn't turned her head as she spoke, so the pain caught her unaware. She moved instinctively, the fingers of her left hand catching the tip of Stone's cigar and dislodging the glowing end. Tears sprang from her eyes at the pain, but she refused to make a sound. She touched the burned spot on the side of her face gingerly and felt the blister that already was rising. Her skin felt raw, as if it'd been scraped away by a dull knife.

"Now you gone an' wrecked my smoke," Stone chuckled. He rode beside her for several strides. "You gotta remember one thing," he said. "You ain't nothin' but a hunk of bait to me—jist a make-sure that your voodoo book man will come after me. That's for true, missy. An' you know I'll kill you if the fancy strikes me, don't you?"

Lee was silent.

"Answer me!"

Her voice was barely a whisper. "I . . . yes. I believe you'd kill me."

"What 'bout you, Mex? You think I'd gun the lady?" His words were rushed now, as if he couldn't spew his evil fast enough. His voice had climbed to an almost feminine pitch, and Lee felt his spittle on her face. Then she heard a whisper of steel touching leather as he drew his pistol.

"*Sí.* You'd kill her, jus' like you say." Pablo's voice seemed far away to Lee. She fixed her eyes to where the barrel of Stone's pistol was jammed against his skull, pushing his thick black hair aside.

"An' what about you, Mex? You think I'd kill you?"

Pablo's voice wavered as he pushed out words. "You have no reason to . . ."

Lee heard Stone take in a deep breath. "I don' need no reason," he said, and suddenly his voice was back to normal.

Pablo's shoulders relaxed slightly. Lee suspected this was not because of Stone's words, but instead the voice he used to deliver them. She swallowed hard and drew a breath.

The spray from the Colt lashed her face with burning bits of black powder. The concussion of the report—not more than eight inches from her ear—threw her off the far side of the horse. She lay there for a moment, numb, not sure whether or not she'd been shot. She looked up. Pablo had been launched forward by the slug, and he slid down his horse's side when the animal reared.

Stone snagged the reins before the frightened horse could bolt. The men who were slightly ahead of the shooting wheeled their horses and raised their pistols and rifles in confusion, seeking the attackers who'd fired on them. Those farther out galloped back to where Stone continued to lead Pablo's horse in a wide circle.

Lee rolled onto her back, both hands covering her face. The screech in her ears was almost unbearable, and louder, somehow, than the actual shot. She winced at the pain in her eyes. It felt as if her eyeballs were being scoured with sand. She resisted the urge to rub them. Instead, she held them both open, letting her tears do their work.

She stared off into the darkness of the prairie for a moment, her vision initially shimmering as if she were looking into the night through an indistinct mist. When she closed her eyes and blinked, she had to grit her teeth to keep from crying out. But at least she could see. And the screeching in her ears was beginning to abate.

She saw that the men were clustered around Stone, who'd dismounted and was now holding Pablo's horse by a single rein. His voice sounded strange to her, barely piercing the racket in her head as he told his gang to take whatever they wanted from the dead man. But, he added, the horse was his. Two of the men dismounted, and then several more followed suit, walking to Pablo's corpse. One of them began hauling off a boot, and another unbuckled the dead man's gun belt.

But no one appeared to be watching her. She eased into a sitting position and began gathering her legs under her. The outlaw she'd embarrassed at the bank had left his horse not fifteen feet from her and was hurrying toward the body.

There was no time to debate, no time to think. She drew breath as she rose to her feet and in a heartbeat was in a full run toward the horse. She snatched the reins, planted her right foot into the left stirrup, and screamed at the startled horse. He reacted precisely as she knew he would—he ran. Outlaws turned at the scream, and a few raised weapons as Lee and the horse crashed through the group like a battering ram, scattering men and horses. Her mount's shoulder took an outlaw in the chest, flinging him at Stone, whose pistol was drawn and beginning its swing toward her. The outlaw took Stone down, and his pistol—or someone else's—fired.

Lee dove at the right side of Pablo's horse, grasping the saddle horn in both hands and using her momentum to arc herself into the saddle. She grabbed the reins. Then she slammed her heels into the horse's sides. The animal responded by plowing through a knot of four or five outlaws as she separated the reins on either side of his neck and gave him his head.

She hadn't yet covered twenty yards when she heard the roar of the Sharp's. The clouds had deserted the moon, and she knew she was too good a target. She wrenched the horse into an impossibly tight turn to the left, ran him hard for a few seconds, and then twisted him into an equally sharp right turn. The roar of the Sharp's was like the thunder of a violent storm. Slugs buzzed past her, some close enough to feel heat.

The horse performed magnificently, responding to Lee's light touch on the reins as she maneuvered him.

A bullet found the saddle horn and whined off into the dark, its impact enough to throw the horse off his stride. He recovered instantly, and, even with death slicing through the cool air around her, Lee rejoiced at the power and coordination of the fine animal.

As they topped a low ridge and began down the far side, she abandoned the twisting and turning and asked—demanded—his all. He stretched out like a cougar at speed, seeming to pull the ground under himself rather than coursing over it. The darkness was her friend, her protector, and she raced into it, ignoring the danger to herself and her horse.

She had no idea in what direction she was headed, but it really made no difference. She was free of Zeb Stone. She leaned forward over her mount's neck and gulped the cool, damp air, like a swimmer breaking the surface after a deep dive. The horse shifted his body slightly as he ran, avoiding obstacles she could barely see until they were past—rocks, clumps of tumbleweed, prairie dog holes. He moved effortlessly, as if he were dancing—dancing in the darkness of the night to a tune only he could hear.

Lee laughed with sheer joy at her freedom and at the speed and coordination of the horse—her horse. As they galloped through the darkened prairie, his new name flashed in her mind. *Night Dancer.*

After she had let Dancer run for a while, she drew rein and let him replenish his lungs with great draughts of air. The buzzing in her ears was barely noticeable now, although the burn from the cigar had begun to throb, and the powder burns from Stone's pistol, no longer cooled by the rush of night air, stung like fresh insect bites on sunburned skin.

She rode on, asking for a gallop when the light was adequate, otherwise holding Dancer to a lope or walk. She wanted to do nothing more than put space between herself and Stone, and she did that for four hours. When she finally stopped, she heard nothing but prairie sounds and saw nothing but indistinct shadows as clouds shifted in front of the moon.

She slid from Dancer's back and adjusted the stirrups to the length of her legs. Then she searched the contents of Pablo's saddlebag. She found a rough cloth, a pair of leather hobbles, a sheathed hunting knife, a few twisted sticks of jerky, and a pistol with one of its grips missing. As she looked at the weapon more closely, she saw that the metal frame that had held the grip was twisted slightly, and its back edge protruded outward in jagged shards of metal. It didn't take a gunsmith to know that a bullet had done the damage. She snapped open the cylinder. There were five bullets in it.

She fit the hobbles at pastern height, and Dancer accepted the restraints calmly. She used the cloth to wipe foam from the horse's neck, chest, and flanks, gnawing at a piece of jerky as she worked. Dancer's breathing had already settled, and his ears followed Lee as she moved around him. When she loosened the girth and let air circulate under the saddle, he grunted contentedly, like a sow rolling in cool mud on a steamy August day.

Then she knelt a few steps away from Dancer and closed her eyes. She thanked God for providing the means of escape and asked earnestly that Stone be stopped from spreading his evil. She'd seen the man's insanity in the bank at Burnt Rock, and again when he killed Pablo. The bizarre swings of his mood, the explosions of his temper, and his wanton cruelty frightened her more than she'd ever been frightened before.

Dancer was watching her, his ears pricked. She walked to his head. The spade bit in his mouth bothered her, and she cringed as her forefinger traced the curve of the shanks. Her fingertips told her that the corners of Dancer's mouth weren't torn—that his saliva had kept them moist—but she knew that the oversized frog in his mouth exerted cruel and needless pressure in response to any movement of the reins. The latigo and leather of the bridle were wet with salty sweat, but she could tell it was a good piece of work—the stitching was straight and tight, and the leather was solid and smooth in her hands.

Lee knew nothing about Dancer other than that he was an exceptional horse and had carried her away from a situation that would have ended in her death. She knew he was intelligent; his interest in the world around him proved that. But could he be trusted? She didn't know that yet, but she had faith in her skills with horses. And something about Dancer told her that they'd already formed the friendship between horse and rider that must exist if the relationship is to be a good one.

She unfastened the bridle and slid the heavy bit out of Dancer's mouth. As she had suspected, the spade bit couldn't be altered by hand. She eased her index finger into the side of Dancer's mouth and moved it gently along the bars, the toothless sections of his lower jawbone. Pressure on the bars could cause instant agony to a horse. Dancer flinched when her finger touched the broken and abraded skin. His tongue felt swollen and slightly puffy to the touch, and she was able to trace scar tissue on it before he twisted his head away.

Lee wondered what to do about the bit. She thought of the Indian-style bitless bridle—a hackamore. She could use that type of bridle to control Dancer not through pain but rather through the touch of the reins against his neck. She had no way of knowing if Dancer had ever been trained to a hackamore, but she went with her instinct. She unfastened the spade bit from the bridle and hurled it out into the scrub.

Then she picked up Pablo's sheath knife. It was heavy in her hands, but the blade was razor sharp. She worked over the bridle as carefully as a surgeon over a patient, cutting leather here, tying it there. She felt little need to hurry her work—she doubted Stone would waste the time attempting a recapture. When she finally looked up from her task, she held in her hand a workable, if not pretty, hackamore. All that remained was to try it on Dancer.

The big horse swung his head away from her when he saw the bridle in her hands. She whispered gentle words, holding the altered bridle to his nostrils. Very gently, she eased the bridle over his muzzle and fitted the back strap behind his ears, smoothing the hairs under the leather. The fit was a good one; the hackamore rested comfortably on his head. Letting the reins hang in front of him, she tied them together near their ends.

Dancer shook his head and snorted, not knowing what to make of the familiar weight of the bridle without the torture of the harsh bit. He shuffled back a couple of steps with the hobble strap tight between his front legs like a too-small belt on a fat man. As she was watching, Lee hummed a monotonous note in an effort to calm the nervous horse.

She watched, not moving at all, seeking the signs that would tell her Dancer was relaxing and beginning to accept the strange new device on his muzzle. Soon, she noticed the slight relaxation of the muscles in his neck and heard the slowing of his breathing. After a half dozen minutes, his ears lost their edgy state of alertness and moved toward Lee almost questioningly. She held her position and continued her humming. After another couple of minutes, Dancer dropped his nose to the dry grass around him and began to munch at it, seeking out green patches. Only then did Lee move to the horse and encircle his neck with her arms. She kissed him below an ear when his head came up. Then, gathering the reins, she climbed into the saddle.

Dancer set out at a walk, shaking his head at the strangeness of the hackamore. Lee eased him into a broad circle to the left, resting the right rein against the right side of his neck, taking up a bit of slack on the left rein. He didn't question the turn, and Lee smiled. She held the reins loosely in her left hand, over the saddle horn, with her little finger taking up slack as needed.

Next, she put Dancer into a canter and reined him through a sweeping figure eight, feeling him pick up the change of leads in the center with the accuracy of a fine watch. The set of his head remained slightly stiff, as if he were expecting to be punished by the old bit at any moment, but he responded beautifully to neck reining—responded so well that Lee realized she couldn't take responsibility for it. Dancer had been trained—perhaps as a cutting and roping horse—before Pablo had owned him. The horse wasn't branded, indicating that he'd been purchased, or more likely stolen, from a breeder or trainer who'd planned to sell him and wanted to avoid a double brand.

Lee asked Dancer for some speed, and he responded with a burst of acceleration that took her breath away. Even after the grueling day yesterday, Dancer launched into a gallop that Lee doubted could be bested by her best short horse. She reined down and stroked her horse's neck, already listing in her mind the mares on her farm she'd breed him to.

But then reality penetrated her bubble of euphoria as she slowed to a walk and checked the sky around her. It would be a long ride to Burnt Rock. And a rumble in her stomach reminded her that she hadn't eaten anything besides jerky in a day, and that Pablo hadn't carried a canteen of water.

But it wasn't the distance or the hunger or the thirst that bothered her—it was the certain knowledge that Ben was riding after Stone to rescue her and bring the outlaws to justice. She'd seen Stone's craziness firsthand, and she knew that he and his gang had no more concern for life than a threatened scorpion. Would Ben come with enough men and firepower to overcome the band of cutthroats and killers?

No, he won't. He'll leave Nick to watch the town, and he'll ride alone.

The sun had drawn away all the moisture from the morning, and heat shimmered in all directions. Lee's stomach growled again as her eyes followed the flight of a red-tailed hawk as it crossed far in front of her, banked, and glided into a landing behind a rise. From the opposite direction, another bird soared in a graceful half circle and swooped downward beyond the rise.

Lee clucked to Dancer and set him ahead at a walk. The heat assaulted her, and she could feel the sweat form on her face. The back of her neck began to tingle, and she eased first one and then another ivory comb from the sloppy, lopsided mess her hair had become. She placed the combs in the saddlebag and ran her fingers through her hair, which fell to her midback and protected her neck from the sun.

She then corrected Dancer's path slightly, pointing him more directly at the rise she could see through the ripples of merciless heat. Another bird circled and then banked downward. She wiped her forehead with the back of her hand. She remembered when she and Ben had ridden south from Burnt Rock last summer, much farther than they'd planned to, and how they'd shared the single canteen they'd brought along. Or so she'd thought until she'd noticed that Ben's throat never moved as he held the canteen to his mouth. She'd reached out and touched his hand with her fingertips, and their eyes had met for a moment. Lee swallowed hard.

He's coming alone.

The scent of water reached Dancer, and he tried to break into a jog. Lee reined him back and held the walk until they reached the oasis. The birds and prairie dogs drinking at the shallow puddle at the base of the rise begrudgingly gave way as Dancer picked a path down the steep face. The water was warm and silty, but that made no difference. She let Dancer suck as much water as he wanted for a couple of minutes and then led him to where a patch of scrub grass had grown in the shade of the rise.

After he'd grazed a bit, she tugged up his head and brought him back to the water. After three such trips, he was happy to forage in the grass, his thirst finally sated. Lee took three pieces of the stone-hard sticks of jerky, soaked them in the puddle while Dancer drank, and gnawed on them as he grazed. The meat was as tasty as a mouthful of wet leather, but after enough chewing, it began to yield some nourishment.

A flash—not even a complete thought—caused her to shiver in spite of the sweat on her forehead and the relentless sun above her. She saw Ben facing Stone and his murderous crew, one man against ten.

"I can help him!" she said loudly enough to cause Dancer to snap his head up and stare at her. "I can help him," she repeated quietly.

She wouldn't go back to Burnt Rock. She would find Ben and ride with him. Dancer and Snorty were both excellent horses; she and Ben would be able to harass the gang without fear of being caught by the outlaws' mounts. She and Dancer could divert the attention of the gang while Ben did the actual damage. She had a quick mind—she'd be a strong ally. It was a good plan.

The idea grew in her mind. She figured the only way they could take Stone would be to pick away at the gang, hitting them at night and riding in and out before the outlaws knew what happened. Maybe strike them twice —or even three times—in the course of a single night. Breed dissension in the gang so they would fight among themselves.

She led Dancer back to the water. He dropped his head to it, sucked for a few seconds, and backed away. Then Lee dropped to her stomach at the edge of the puddle, forced herself to swallow several mouthfuls, and stood. Ben, she figured, wasn't far from her. He'd probably ridden through the night just as she and the gang had. She wasn't sure of the directions, but east and west were always clear. Stone had said he was headed west toward the border. She'd simply ride long sweeps first north and then swing back south, until she saw Ben or he saw her. The immensity of the prairie began to push into her consciousness like a dark cloud over a church picnic, but she chased the thought before it could settle and do any damage.

She mounted and turned Dancer toward another, steeper rise that shimmered in the heat a few miles from them. *I'll have a decent vantage point from there. And maybe I'll find Ben right away!*

Lee came to some water at dusk, when the harsh sun had faded and the edges of things were becoming softer and less distinct. She was in great need of a rest. Her blouse stuck to her back as if it were glued with library paste, and her hair hung in knotted clumps, adhering to the sweat on her face. Her throat was so dry that she couldn't generate enough saliva to wet her lips, which were swollen from the constant sun. Her stomach was growling, and at one point in the day, she'd dozed in the saddle for a few minutes and dreamed of beef stew with buttermilk biscuits and a glass of sweet tea made with icy branch water. The backs of her hands and her face were burned red, and she had a sun blister on the end of her nose. Her other blister, from Stone's cigar, weeped liquid down her cheek and throbbed with her pulse. And Dancer had become cranky and fought for his head every so often, weary of the snail's pace and wanting to cover some ground to get somewhere—anywhere—away from the sun.

She slid down Dancer's side and fell to her knees in the water. Blessedly cool, the tiny pond was fed by an underground spring. She splashed her face and hair while Dancer submerged his muzzle and drank next to her. When she stood, she looked down at herself in the waning light. Her once-white blouse was stained with sweat and dirt, and her skirt looked as if it had been dragged behind her rather than worn. Her shoes were dried, grayish husks, and the soles were separating from the uppers.

After cooling herself in the water, she sank to the ground, too exhausted to think clearly. She hadn't found Ben, she was terribly hungry and sore, and she had nothing to feed her horse. She was quite sure that things couldn't be much worse.

In the distance, she thought she heard thunder. She listened intently, eyes closed, and heard it again.

5

Ben had killed men before, so he wasn't surprised by the complete exhaustion that covered him like a heavy, suffocating blanket when the adrenaline in his system receded. More than anything else, he wanted to sleep, to refresh his body and ease the pain that was throbbing on the side of his head where the rifle bullet had come within an inch of ending his life. He wanted to let sleep wash from his mind the image of the bloody corpse on the ground.

Instead, he replaced the spent cartridges in his pistols, taking the fresh shells from the loops in his gun belt and sliding them into the cylinders, giving no thought to the process. The smell of burned gunpowder clung stubbornly to his hands and his shirt and vest, and the stench made the jerky and water in his stomach churn and climb hotly into his throat.

After a few minutes, the shifting and thinning of the cloud cover gave Ben enough light to do what he needed to do. He stripped the stock saddle and bridle from the outlaw's horse and smacked the animal on the rump. The horse broke into a run without a look back, and his hoofbeats resounded in the still air for what seemed like a very long time. Ben searched through the saddlebags and transferred some of what he found to his own bags. The sack of Arbuckle's coffee brought a tired grin to his face. The can of sliced peaches in heavy syrup was an unexpected treat. He found a small paper sack that held the gunman's supply of *hempa* and a few packages of rolling papers, but he upended the bag and scattered the contents on the ground. He put a block of lucifers into his vest pocket and untied a slicker from the saddle and put it behind his own. A fourteen-inch, straight-bladed knife he found had a razor edge, was well oiled, and fit snugly into a deerskin sheath. He attached this to his gun belt behind the pistol on his left side. He practiced pulling it a few times until his fingers and palm automatically found the bone grip of the knife. Then he turned to the corpse.

The outlaw was sprawled on his back, one arm outstretched, the other across his chest. Ben drew the man's pistol. It was a Smith & Wesson .45 revolver that even in the weak light showed rust and lack of maintenance. He tossed it aside. He saw a gold chain that indicated a pocket watch rested in the man's vest pocket. He left it there. He considered the bandoleer, but it was blood soaked and foul. He found the rifle eight or ten feet from the body. It seemed sound; he worked the action, and the mechanism clicked smoothly. He tied it over the dead man's slicker on Snorty's saddle.

Not far from the rifle, Ben found an unlabeled quart bottle of whiskey. He took the bandana from around his neck, doused it thoroughly with whiskey, and pressed it to the wound on his head. Staggering with the pain, he felt as if he'd been touched with a white-hot branding iron. When the feeling began to diminish, he wrung out the bandana, saturated it again, and repeated the process. A groan escaped through his clenched teeth.

After the third time, he pitched the bottle far out into the prairie, sat shakily on the ground, and tried to clear his mind. He had no idea how close the rest of the gang might be, or if they'd swing back to check on this outlaw when he failed to rejoin them with Ben as his prisoner. Would Stone turn from being the pursued to the pursuer in order to avenge his dead henchman? Unlikely. The death of the outlaw who lay a few feet from Ben would only put more money in the pot for the others.

Ben shook his head and immediately regretted it. The throbbing of his wound had lessened a bit when he'd sat down, but the quick movement brought it back again with almost stunning power. He decided to rest for another moment and then move on.

As he climbed into his saddle a few minutes later, he saw that the sky to the east was beginning to lose some darkness as the pastels of early morning pushed up into the horizon. He hadn't watered Snorty, but he didn't intend to be riding long.

As he rode away, the dead man he'd left behind and unburied preyed on his mind. He'd snuffed out the life of another human being—another one of God's children—and the enormity of what he'd done awed and frightened him. He couldn't push away the questions. How much of his relentless dogging of Stone was about his concern over Lee? How much was generated by his sinful desire for revenge against the man who'd murdered his father? Was he truly doing the job he was called to do, or was he simply bent on killing another man?

Of course it's Lee. His feelings for her were strong and ran deep. He'd give his life to rescue her from Stone if that were required.

One hour later, Ben put tentative fingers to his wound. Most of it was crusted over with dried blood, but a bit of fluid seeped in a couple of places. The gouge continued to transmit shattering jolts of pain throughout his head whenever Snorty sidestepped a rock or a patch of tall scrub.

He held the exploring fingers in front of his face and squinted at them. The liquid appeared to be clear, which was good, but its putrid odor made him gag, which could be very bad. He wondered if he'd been too quick to use the outlaw's whiskey as a disinfectant. The unlabeled bottle flickered in his mind. Properly distilled liquor worked just fine, but Mexican booze was often made from rotten fruit, wormy corn, and whatever else happened to be around the still. He'd been told by a *vaquero* once that it was a common practice to toss a butchered hog's head or a couple of dead rats into the vat to speed up fermentation. The thought made him cringe.

Ben hardly noticed the sun clearing the horizon. Riding the foothills took his attention, and he was finding it increasingly difficult to concentrate and guide Snorty around obstacles. Copses of trees lay ahead, but they seemed to move along with him so that he never got any closer. He considered taking off his shirt and vest, and then wondered at the stupidity of such a notion. Where had it come from? If he did that, the sun would bake him like a suckling pig on a spit in a matter of a few hours. He couldn't recall being so hot this early in the morning before. And there was a strange buzzing sound in both his ears, as if an insect was trapped inside his head.

There was something terribly wrong. He swung from a state of near exhaustion and wrenching pain to a state of bizarre euphoria—and then back to the depths. Sweat sheeted his face, and his body was on fire. But then his teeth chattered, and his entire frame trembled with shivers. His vision was distorted. And he was scared—almost terrified—but he didn't know the cause of the fear. It seemed to encompass him like a cloud.

When a jackrabbit bolted from under a skunkbush, Ben drew his Colt and opened fire. Spurts of dirt sprang up near the rabbit, some within a few inches of it, others several feet away. He fired until the hammer clicked hollowly on empty cartridges. Snorty began to pitch and spin, and Ben pawed clumsily at his saddle horn. The sun set in a fraction of a second, and a thick darkness enveloped him.

He looked around. The sun was back. He was sitting on the ground for some reason, and he had no idea how he'd gotten there. Snorty nickered behind him, but he could hardly hear through the constant droning in his ears. He was hotter than he'd ever been, hotter than when he'd been ten hours out of Lubbock, when the horse he was riding spooked at a snake and threw him, and he'd had to walk back. Late in that day, he'd seen a lake not far ahead of him and had run toward it, but didn't get any closer. He'd fallen, gotten up, fallen again, and gotten up again—and then stayed down the next time he dropped. The miner's mule had hee-hawed at him, and it sounded like the back door of the barn Pa never got around to oiling the hinges on, and the old man—the miner—had come along and said there wasn't any lake and that . . .

Ben struggled to consciousness through the crazy images and the buzzing in his head. He found that he was facedown in a stilted patch of scrub. He knew he needed water. It was hard to think or to remember where he was, but he knew he had to have some water. When he tried to stand, the ground moved under his boots. He wanted water. He needed water. There was water in his saddlebags, canteens full of it.

Where is Snorty?

He slept again, for an hour—or a minute or half a week. He didn't know. His horse was gone. He had no water. He must have water soon or he'd die.

When Snorty's muzzle touched the back of his neck, he screamed, and the horse reared in panic. Ben found himself on his knees, fighting for balance. In a moment he fell back on his seat, legs askew in front of him. Snorty cautiously approached again, huffing through his nostrils. Ben knew that if he scared his horse again, he might never get close enough to grab a rein or a stirrup.

He knew what he needed to do. Whether or not he could do it was the question. He didn't dare stand, or even reach out—the awkward, uncoordinated action of his body would be frighteningly unfamiliar to the animal. He didn't want the confused horse to run away.

He attempted to slide himself around to face Snorty's side, since the horse was standing directly behind him. The animal flinched as Ben was forced to push out a hand and arm to keep himself from falling. Snorty's left stirrup was less than two feet from where his right hand was planted against the soil. Even if he snagged the stirrup, he knew there was the chance that Snorty would panic and bolt. Still, the familiar weight in the stirrup and the sense of being handled and controlled could take over, and he might manage to get to his feet and reach into a saddlebag for a canteen.

He had no choice. He tried his voice, hoping it didn't sound as raspy and distorted to Snorty as it did to himself. Words were too hard to form, but he could hum a single note—a fairly low note—that the horse might find comforting. Lee had taught him that . . . when?

He waited until the dizziness was about to claim him again and then pulled his hand from the ground and stuck it through the stirrup, grabbing the leathers as tightly as he could. Snorty jerked back slightly and then stood stock still, as if the feeble pressure Ben was exerting could hold him in place. Using the stirrup as a support, Ben pulled himself awkwardly to his knees and then to his feet. With his left hand in a death grip on the saddle horn, he pawed through the saddlebag with his right hand and dragged out a canteen. Pulling the cork with his teeth, he drank deeply, letting the tepid water flow into his parched mouth and throat and down into his gut.

The water brought some clarity to his mind, and he looked around. Ahead stood a copse of stunted trees, which meant there was both water and shade there. Ben knew he couldn't stay where he was; if he fell and slept again, he wouldn't live to see the next day. The sun would squeeze every drop of moisture from his body.

He draped the canteen cord around his neck and extended his right arm and hand to the far side of the saddle, keeping his hold on the saddle horn with his left. He gathered what little strength he had and tried to boost himself high enough to get his left boot into the stirrup. His legs were weak—his attempt succeeded only in raising him to his toes. He knew that, at best, he had one more try in him; if he failed this time, his strength would be gone. Quickly, before he could think it over, he shoved against the ground with his right foot and picked up his left, poking the toe of his boot to where the stirrup should be. His arms and shoulders screamed at him as he hung on to the saddle with all the strength he had. His boot brushed the stirrup aside once, and then again. He was beginning to slide lower on Snorty's side—his grip was weakening. Then he felt his boot brush leather. With his final speck of strength, he commanded his arms to drag him up a few inches higher. *Please, God . . .*

The sensation of the sole of his boot against the rough leather inside the stirrup was one of the most beautiful things Ben had ever felt. Hauling his right leg up and over Snorty's side and back was another battle, one that brought a groan of effort from deep inside him. When he finally slumped in the saddle, both hands grasping the saddle horn, his arms trembled with exhaustion. He leaned forward at the waist to grab a rein and welded the other to the horn. He repeated the move for the other rein and then urged Snorty ahead with the most leg pressure he could manage.

He crouched in his saddle, disorienting peaks of dizziness stealing his balance. Black specks drifted randomly in his vision and began to move faster, soon swarming like dark snowflakes in a winter storm. In his head was a constant, discordant buzz he couldn't escape. The water he'd drunk so rapidly rode up in his throat, and the sun pounded at him, its cruel fingers jabbing at the raw channel above his ear. Images in his fevered mind appeared and disappeared quickly, until a scene that was etched into his very being played itself out in front of him.

A saloon built from unpainted scrap wood stood beside a ramshackle mercantile that threatened to collapse at any moment. A hand-painted sign over the sagging batwings of the saloon announced simply "Cerveza." An unrecognizable melody from an out-of-tune guitar drifted into the ovenlike heat of the street. A couple of mules were tied to the hitching post, along with three lathered saddle horses carrying good-quality American stock saddles.

Ben looped his reins over the short hitching rail and walked toward the saloon. Halfway there, he crouched and picked up a handful of the fine, dusty powder of the street and sifted it from one hand to another. Then he lifted each of his Colts up by their grips to the point where only the last inch of the barrels remained inside the holster. When he released the weapons, they settled into the tanned and shaped leather in precisely the position he needed them to be.

From the street he could see that the inside of the saloon was as dark as a cave. He'd ridden around the place earlier. There was a glassless window on one side of the narrow building and a back door that hung at an angle from a single hinge. A few lanterns hung from the walls at night, but in the daytime the only light came from the window and doors and through the poorly caulked gaps between the boards of the structure.

He approached the front batwings at an angle, giving his eyes as much opportunity to adjust as he could. From his place on the warped wooden sidewalk, he could see a pair of prostitutes leaning against the bar, close to the front. A vaquero was slouched toward the middle of the bar, his sombrero hanging on his back. He had a bottle of whiskey in front of him and a glass in his hand. Beyond the Mexican stood Zeb Stone, talking to a man who had bandoleers of ammunition crossed over his chest.

"Stone."

Stone turned to face him. "Well," he said. "Well."

Ben concentrated all his senses on Stone. The outlaw moved a step away from the bar, flexing the fingers of both hands, which were at waist level in front of him. His eyes were clear, and it looked like he'd shaved that morning. Ben flicked his eyes to Stone's hands. They were as calm as the hands of a statue.

"You know who I am, don't you?" Ben said.

"I know. Let's git to it." Stone's mouth started to form another word and then his hands flashed toward the grip of his pistol.

Time broke into fragments for Ben. Stone's draw seemed jerky, as if it stopped and started a hundred times before his own fingertips grazed the grips of his guns. His pistols somehow raised and extended, their barrels pointed at Stone's midsection. He wasn't completely sure how they'd gotten there. He watched, as if from a seat in a theater, as the hammers of the .45s in his hands slid back and began their downward arc. It seemed like an age before the hammers were home, but the impact of the two bullets an inch above Stone's belt buckle was instantaneous, as was the gush of blood and the crumpling of Stone's body to the floor. The outlaw's pistol had not cleared leather.

Ben stared at the well of blood pumping from Stone's midsection before he holstered his pistol.

"Might just as well finish him off. Gut-shot death is a long time coming," the Mexican said.

"The way I hear it, he wasn't in a hurry to let my pa die."

"Up to you."

Ben didn't reply. Stone moved on the floor and then groaned. His hands reached for his stomach as if trying to stop the flow of blood. Ben turned away, moved past the Mexican, and left the saloon. He swung into his saddle and put several miles between him and the sordid little town before he thought about what he'd done.

When the uncontrollable shivering started . . .

Ben's frame jangled as ague sent its frigid tendrils through his body. It took him a moment to realize that Snorty had stopped and had his head down, sucking scum-covered water from a shallow water hole half the size of a wagon bed. There was shade here, he saw, and a covering of sparse grass around the water hole. He dismounted slowly, fighting dizziness, and when both his boots were on the ground, he reached under Snorty and pulled the cinch free. The bit and bridle stayed where they were; the bit was low-ported and Snorty could graze freely with it in his mouth. Ben hauled the saddle and blanket off his horse's back, but his legs crumpled under the weight, and he fell next to the water.

As he lay on the ground, he noticed a group of desert pine standing six feet away, and the secure, foot-high space under their lowest branches looked as inviting as a canopy bed in the finest hotel. He crawled toward the trees, dragging the sweat-soaked saddle blanket with him. By the time he made it to the shade, fever had replaced the arctic chill with the heat of a flash fire. With the last of his strength, he dragged himself under the lowest branches of the nearest tree and collapsed, still clutching the saddle blanket. When he awoke, it was night. He pulled the blanket over himself as best he could and slept again.

The first thing he noticed when he woke up was that the noise inside his head was gone. Pain from his wound was still with him, but it was a cleaner, more bearable pain, one that reached him directly rather than being filtered through disorientation and fever.

The second thing he noticed was that he smelled terrible; a fetid combination of dried blood, fever sweat, and the poisons draining from his body created a cloud of long-dead animal odor around him. He crawled out from under the branches and checked the position of the sun—half a day was gone. He sat in the warmth for a few minutes and then began to remove his clothing, setting his gun belt, leather vest, and boots aside. Clutching his clothes and the saddle blanket to his chest, he stood and walked unsteadily. The weakness in his legs reminded him that he wasn't completely over whatever had gotten to him.

He stopped at the edge of the water hole. Snorty had muddied the water when he stood in it to drink, but that made no particular difference to Ben. He moved to the center of the pool, where the water barely reached his waist, and sat down, pressing his bundle of clothes below the surface. The water was tepid and covered with green scum—and felt wonderful. He swished his denim pants back and forth, wrung them out, and washed them again before tossing them back to the shore. His shirt, bandana, socks, underdrawers, and saddle blanket received the same treatment. Then he put his head and chest below the surface and stayed there until his breath ran out. He used a handful of sand to rub his skin in lieu of soap and parted the pond scum with his hands as he strode to the shore. The sun dried his body quickly as he hung his clothes from branches to dry.

He gave Snorty the rest of the crimped oats, leaned back against a tree, and slept again.

Zebulon Stone spat into the fire in front of him. It was down to white embers now, perfect to cook the rabbits his men had killed earlier in the day. He lifted a bottle and took a long, gurgling drink from its neck. The *pulque,* a raw-distilled whiskey made from cactus, burned his throat like molten steel. He knew the burning would be even more intense when the whiskey reached his stomach, where things had never completely healed since Flood had put the slugs in him. He spat into the fire and again lifted the bottle to his mouth.

The men—except the three he'd posted as lookouts—were drunk and loud on the *pulque*. Shots rang out every so often as they fired into the sky, and the occasional thunderclap of the Sharp's made the pistol reports sound like popcorn. Stone grinned. They were his blood brothers: night riders, thieves, rapists, killers—none of whom he would trust any farther than he could throw a bull buffalo. Not a one of them had any more regard for human life than a coyote, which made them perfect underlings in his gang of misfits. Because they feared him, they obeyed him, and because they obeyed him, they were richer than they'd ever believed they could be. Their loyalty to him or to anyone else except themselves was nonexistent, but their greed and their unquenchable thirst for violence and blood kept them in line.

He had gunned down three of his men in the last few months, each of them in front of the gang. The disputes had been either minor, manufactured by him, or simply without reason, as in Pablo's case, but they achieved what the outlaw leader wanted. The survivors were sufficiently impressed by his insanity and wanted to keep on his good side.

An outlaw wearing the torn and dirty gray shirt and pants of the Confederate army hunkered down next to his boss. "Been two days now. I guess Georgie ain't comin' back," he said.

"No loss. Half the time he was stupid on that weed of his, an' the rest of the time he was stupid on booze. Flood done us a favor."

"You figure he killed him?"

"Georgie woulda been back by now if he was alive. He wouldn't go too far from his share of the money."

"Thing is, Zeb," the man began hesitantly, "we're doin' real good. We can hole up in Mexico for as long as we want an' still have all the money we need. Why not just forgit about Flood? We could—"

"Lemme tell you somethin', Reb. Flood's more important to me than the money or any of you bunch of scum." He took a pull at the bottle and wiped his mouth with his sleeve. "You ever been left for dead by a Bible-totin' coward? You ever felt the fire in your gut a couple of slugs can put there? You ever wanted to die jist to git away from the pain? That coward ambushed me like I was some stinkin' rummy that sweeps the floors an' cleans out the spittoons in a fleabag Mex saloon an' is caught with his paw in the till. You ever feel anything like that?"

"I didn't mean nothin', Zeb. You got ever' right to—"

Stone's words spilled out faster. "I got me the town picked out, an' this time it's gonna be a fair fight—an' Flood an' his voodoo book are goin' down to stay. I'm gonna watch him draw his last breath an' laugh like I was at a Fourth of July picnic!"

"Sure, Zeb. An' I'll back you up ever' step of the way! Ain't no man who can ambush Zeb Stone an' live to tell—"

The click of Stone's hammer being drawn back ended the man's fawning as quickly and completely as would a bullet to his brain. He hadn't seen Stone draw. Beyond the fire, a spatter of pistol fire and drunken whoops erupted. After a long moment, Stone eased the hammer down and holstered his pistol.

"Git me another bottle," he said, "an' I'll let you live a little longer."

When the sun passed its zenith and started downward, the slight drop in temperature roused Ben from the deep sleep in which he'd spent the day. As he dressed in his dry and fresh-smelling clothes, he realized he wasn't sure how long he'd slept. It was possible, he knew, that he'd been out for better than twenty-four hours. And he wasn't sure how long he'd been sick. Two days? Longer?

He smiled as he noticed a sensation he hadn't experienced since before he'd ridden out of Burnt Rock: He was very, very hungry.

6

The pistol with the missing grip felt like an unfamiliar tool in Lee's hands as she followed the erratic meandering of a jackrabbit with the sight at the end of the barrel. The fractured metal, probably the result of the grip being shot off in a gunfight, dug into the base of her thumb. Sweat dripped into her right eye—her aiming eye—but she didn't dare move to wipe it away. The sun weighted on her like a bearskin robe, and its rays glinted off the places on the barrel where the bluing had worn away and pierced her eyes like tiny needles.

The jackrabbit dug at something with its forepaws and put its head down to sniff at the bit of root. Lee's finger began a slow, even pressure on the trigger, with the sight at the juncture of the animal's head and neck. She'd cocked the hammer of the single-action Colt a couple hours ago and hadn't yet fired.

She pushed away the possibility that the weapon could explode in her face when she pulled the trigger. If the barrel had been at all damaged in Pablo's gunfight, she was holding in her hand what amounted to a stick of dynamite with a burning fuse. She concentrated again on the rabbit. The sweat burned in her eye, but she fought against the blink that was causing her eyelid to twitch. The animal turned toward her, and its dark eyes moved past her without stopping. She applied a butterfly's breath more pressure, moving the sight to the white crest on the rabbit's chest, and drew a breath through slightly parted lips.

The rabbit skittered behind a rock, out of her line of fire. A second later a red-tailed hawk swooped in from her right, its talons extended and beak open, a chilling *screeeeee* issuing from its throat. It took less than a heartbeat; the rabbit screamed as the hawk's claws sank into it, and then the bird rose sharply with its claws locked into the rabbit's spine.

Lee eased the hammer forward to its seated position and stood, wiping her eyes with her left hand. Wobbling a bit on her feet, she tried to see past the dark specks that floated before her eyes. She'd not slept the night before. The storm had soaked her, and the sharp wind that followed the thunder, rain, and lightning had chilled her so deeply that her teeth continued to chatter uncontrollably until well after the sun had risen.

Dancer snorted, and when she looked over at him, he was eyeing her with curiosity. He wasn't thirsty; he'd been sucking water from holes and depressions through the day and into the afternoon. But grazing was sparse. He chewed at the brown, almost lifeless prairie grass without much interest.

The Busted Backs were visible in the distance, even through the shimmering waves of heat. To her west, she could barely discern the shapes of what might be a few trees—probably scrubby desert pines, but at least they'd yield some shade. She thought she could make it there easily, but she also knew that distances were deceiving on the open prairie. *What if that little spot is a day's ride or more from where I stand?* The more she stared, the farther away the trees seemed to be. *There's water there, or the trees couldn't grow,* she thought. *And some animals or birds must drink the water. If only the gun would shoot straight . . .*

It was the gun that worried her. She had confidence in her own marksmanship. Uncle Noah had taught her a great deal about survival in the West. Her shooting lessons had begun when she was ten, and she had to use both hands to hold the small, single-shot .22 caliber Derringer. By the time she was fourteen, she could put six slugs into a saucer-sized circle painted on an old board fifty feet away. When she was sixteen, Uncle Noah introduced her to rifles, and she showed as much skill with long guns as she did with pistols.

She'd never gone hunting with Uncle Noah, although much of the meat they ate came strapped over the back of his stoutest stallion. She'd told her uncle, "When I'm starving—when I *really* need the food and have no other way to get it—I'll go hunting."

Right now, on her third day without eating, she really needed the food. Hunger was draining her strength, and she knew she had to be alert in order to find Ben.

It was almost dark when she reached the water hole. The place had seemed to travel away from her at the same speed at which she'd approached it. And she hadn't dared ask Dancer to hurry; he'd eaten nothing of substance for two days, and his stomach roiled and growled with hunger. When he'd caught the scent of grass, he fought her, but she'd held him at a walk all the way, talking and humming to keep him calm.

By the time she'd stripped off the saddle and rubbed him down with handfuls of dried weeds, it was almost too dark to see. She fit the hobbles on the horse mostly by touch while he happily chomped away at the patches of green grass near the trees.

After seeing to Dancer, she settled under the saddle blanket with her back against the saddle and the pistol in her right hand. As she said her prayers and drifted into sleep, her stomach growled monotonously, like a far-off thunderstorm.

The noise, a skittering sort of sound, drew her from her sleep. She gathered her thoughts before she eased her eyes open. Hunger had been her first conscious thought—and her second thought was that whatever was making the noise could no doubt be eaten. Her grip tightening on the pistol, she raised her eyelids the slightest bit and stared at the water hole through tiny slits. A couple of prairie dog families—several adults and twice as many young ones—were arguing on the far side of the water, perhaps fifteen feet from her. The animals moved rapidly, seeming to leap or run for no reason.

An impossible shot. Her breath left her in a long sigh, and she began to push back the saddle blanket when she heard Dancer scuffle in the grass beyond a trio of pines. As she swung her head to the sound, she saw a jackrabbit darting between two of the trees, switching directions, and then scrambling in a straight line that would bring it past her not more than six or eight feet away.

Her left hand was already on the edge of the blanket; she brought it toward her feet and raised the .38. "Target shooting's for easterners," Uncle Noah had told her. "Instinct shooting's what puts meat on the table."

The jackrabbit veered again, away from her. She swung the pistol in a smooth, short arc and squeezed the trigger. The eruption of dirt in front of the animal caused it to veer again, toward her, and she squeezed the trigger a second time. The rabbit took the slug in its chest, did a loose backward somersault, and flopped to the dirt on its side. Its rear legs twitched twice, and then the body was still.

Lee stood and walked the few steps to her kill. She'd never cleaned a rabbit for the pot—but that really didn't matter. She had no pot, and she had no fire. Bile rose to the back of her throat as she pictured eating the raw meat, but she knew she had no choice. She cut out slabs of side meat and two legs, washed the meat in the water hole, and ate until she was past full.

She slept then in the shade of the desert pines. When she awakened, most of the day was gone. She felt stronger and cooler—much better than before she'd eaten.

All of Stone's men had hangovers when he woke them up that morning by firing the Sharp's into the remains of the fire. The thumb-sized slug hit the embers and sent sparks and bits of wood fifteen feet into the sky. Then the debris of the fire settled on the men like raindrops from a passing cloud—except that this rain was hot and burned their flesh, hair, and clothes.

"Fill your canteens," Stone ordered as he paced around the camp with the big rifle over his shoulder, his finger still inside the trigger guard. "We ain't stoppin' today, 'cept to give the horses a breather, an' we ain't stoppin' tonight. We can't afford to kill the crowbait we're ridin', so we'll walk 'em until the heat lets up. Any of you who has a horse drop out from under you walks, an' the money stays with the gang—with me—until you catch up an' claim it." He smiled for a moment. "'Course, that ain't real likely to happen."

He set the Sharp's on the ground next to his saddle and took a cigar from his pocket. He scratched the head of a lucifer with his thumbnail, lit the stogie, and continued his pacing. "We got five, maybe six days of ridin' to get to where we're goin'. Where that is, is a smelly little Mex town called LaRosa, maybe twenty miles over the border. There's a saloon there that's jist perfect for me to meet Flood in." He paused to look over the gang.

"See, that's what all this is about: Me meetin' Ben Flood. Anybody got questions?"

"S'pose Flood meets up with his woman an' rides back to his town with his tail 'tween his legs?" said a buffalo of a man with bandoleers crisscrossing his barrel chest. "What happens then?"

Stone spat into the dirt as if the comment had brought a foul taste to his mouth. "Ain't gonna happen. Me an' Flood's gonna meet in that saloon—only this time, I'm the one who's gonna walk out." Ten pairs of reddened eyes fixed on him as he took a long drag on his cigar. "Saddle up. We got ground to cover."

The men began to move, pulling on boots, draining the final drops out of bottles discarded the night before, rolling cigarettes, moving shakily toward their horses.

"Hold on, gents," Stone called out. "I forgot to mention a couple of things. There's a girls' school in LaRosa run by a buncha nuns, and in the next town 'bout a dozen miles away, there's a bank that'll be like swipin' candy from a baby—an' since the war ended, the Mexicans aren't tradin' in nothin' but silver an' gold."

A hoarse cheer had begun when Stone mentioned the convent school, and the news about the bank doubled the volume. The men moved faster, their hangovers all but forgotten.

Stone smiled to himself. The fact that there wasn't a bank within two hundred miles of LaRosa made no difference to him. His followers would be satisfied with what they found at the school and in the saloon. There probably weren't ten men in LaRosa who owned a weapon, and those few would go down first as his gang took over the town. He smiled at the thought.

Lee slept away the hottest part of the day. Then she saddled up and rode to a nearby ridge. Dancer scrambled up the slope as if he'd been bred to it, his rear hooves flinging stones and dirt behind him like a dog digging up a favorite buried bone. Now that the heat of the day had given up and was replaced by a gentle evening breeze, it seemed to Lee that the Busted Backs had taken gigantic strides across the prairie toward her. The peaks of the hills were sharp, delineated crisply by the last light of day.

She stood in her stirrups and looked out over the vastness. Ben had told her that there were two ways through the Busted Backs—one an easy passage but slow, and the other hard and often dangerous but much quicker. Ben, she knew, would take the faster route—or maybe he'd already taken it. If so, waiting on this side of the range of low mountains would accomplish nothing.

Ben would be coming soon. She knew it.

The night was a cool one; she wrapped herself in her saddle blanket and pulled her knees up to her chest to conserve body heat. Coyotes howled to one another, the plaintive clarity of their cries echoing over the prairie. The sound carried without distortion through the night air, and its melancholy texture made her feel completely alone. She prayed silently that the Lord would rid her of the nugget of panic beginning to form in her heart.

Ben sighed with satisfaction. The snake had been large enough—as thick as his forearm—that the ribs were like darning needles and served as superior toothpicks. The skin, with its familiar dusty brown and pale yellow diamond shapes, was buried not far from where he had built the fire. He gave little credence to the old superstition that if a dead rattler, or its skin, was left unburied, its mate would seek it out that night and take revenge on its killer. Still, an Indian friend had told him that snakes had excellent senses of smell; in fact, they located their meals through both smell and by the heat the prey exuded. Didn't it make sense that a rattler could identify the scent of its mate—dead or alive—and seek it out?

Fat dripped from the chunks of meat spitted on a desert pine sucker, and the embers flared. Tongues of flame touched the meat, which had already turned from pure white to a light, golden brown. Water boiled in the peach can; Ben added a parsimonious handful of the ground coffee, watched the boiling water for a moment, and tossed in another handful. Within a few minutes, the scent of coffee surrounded him, hanging in the still night air like a fragrant cloud.

When the coffee was ready, he manipulated the can from the fire using a pair of sticks and set it aside to cool. It wasn't that he didn't enjoy his coffee burning hot; rather, he couldn't touch the can without raising blisters the size of gold eagles on his fingers. He gnawed at the rattlesnake, grunting at the rich, gamy flavor of the meat, while grease ran down the thickening stubble on his chin. He ate until the skewer was empty, then threw it aside and touched a tentative fingertip to the can, finding he could hold it for short periods of time. The coffee was thick and strong but not bitter, and he sipped at it until both the can and the liquid had cooled enough for him to take longer, more satisfying draughts. He settled back on one elbow, swirling his coffee in the can, and gave his mind over to the life-and-death situation that had started at the Burnt Rock Land and Trust Company.

Ben didn't consider himself a complicated man; he knew he was neither a theologian nor an academic. He viewed himself as a Christian, a marshall, a good friend to those he cared about, and a man to whom money meant little. His plans—concerning both his work and his life in general—were simple ones. His course, now, was neat and unembellished: to find Stone and his gang, free Lee, and bring the outlaws to justice. Facing them was foolish—almost suicidal. The odds were insane. He'd have to mount his attacks at night, and he'd have to move as quickly and as quietly as a nocturnal bird of prey. But his first priority was to free Lee. He couldn't begin his assault on the outlaws until she was free and headed back to Burnt Rock.

He sat up and set the empty can aside. He found that his shoulders had grown tight and tense and his palms had become slightly damp. *Maybe I'd better get Lee free before I even think about what comes next. God knows what's supposed to happen—and he'll let me know when the time is right.* Under Snorty's saddle blanket, he prayed for guidance until he fell asleep.

He woke at first light. The crystal-like clarity of the still-cool air was invigorating and delicious. He coaxed a tiny flame from the remains of the previous night's fire and fed it with twigs and kindling, filled the peach can with water, and set it on the flame. Before long the water was churning, and he rained coffee into it.

He wasn't sure how much time he'd lost. He had to make up that time, he knew, and he couldn't do it at night. Travel then was too unsure; the moon was growing smaller each evening. With cloud cover filtering what little moonlight there was, any gait faster than a walk was a potential disaster. He gazed off toward the Busted Backs, their peaks and foothills sharply visible in the morning air.

He kicked dirt over his fire and saddled Snorty. When he mounted, the animal launched into a series of feel-good hops, bucked a couple of times, and was ready to stretch when Ben nudged him with the heels of his boots. They ran at breakneck speed over the prairie; when Ben reined in two miles closer to the Busted Backs, Snorty was ready to cover ground at whatever pace was asked for. Ben settled into a walk-jog-lope-gallop sequence.

It felt good to be riding with a clear head, to not feel the impact of each hoof in his wound. The furrow on the side of his skull was mending well. The wound was dry, and the scab over it was thick yet slightly supple, moving easily with any motions of his head.

A hunch told him that something important was going to happen that day, and he had learned long ago to trust his hunches. He didn't know if the event would be good or bad, but he knew it was coming. He drew the rifle from his scabbard and checked its load, even though he'd done that earlier before riding out. He drew his pistol while Snorty was at a walk and spun its cylinder.

Soon the heat was pouring from the sky like lava. He stopped and held his Stetson full of canteen water in front of Snorty's muzzle, looking forward to putting the wet hat back on his head. Suddenly he saw a vague line of trail dust in the distance. He mounted and stood in his stirrups, but the foothills and ridges between him and the line of dust blocked his vision. He figured it was a drifter or a traveler—a peddler, maybe—heading for the short route over the Busted Backs. It could even be a mustang or two that'd been run off from their main herd and were wandering the prairie.

Or it could be another outlaw looking for him—either simply for observation, or to bring him back to Zeb Stone. *But why would Stone send out another man? He must realize by now that I killed his first watchdog. But Stone doesn't think at all like a normal man.*

Ben watched the trail of grit inch its way toward the far horizon. He and the other rider were approaching one another as if they were riding to the apex of a wide triangle, each of them beginning from a separate base. Although it was hard to gauge distance through the waves of shimmering heat, he figured their paths would intersect before dark. Until then, there was nothing to do but press on toward the Busted Backs.

Lee kept her eyes on the sky. The rider she saw couldn't be Ben—Ben would already be ahead of her, perhaps into the range of low mountains. But the unseen horseman might be someone who could give her some food or perhaps some more ammunition for her pistol. Of course, he could be a saddle tramp, in which case there'd be trouble. She was glad Pablo hadn't discarded his damaged weapon.

It looked as if the two paths would intersect later that day. She was hungry again, but she decided she couldn't spare a bullet—not until she found out who her uninvited companion was.

An afternoon breeze had long since scattered the dust trails in the sky and whisked away and diffused new ones. Ben was growing increasingly nervous. As much as he told himself that the other rider—if that's what it was—was innocent, a hunch told him something else.

In the late afternoon, he came upon a water hole and stripped off Snorty's tack, untying the dead outlaw's rifle from behind the cantle. He'd adjusted his path slightly while still on horseback, cutting more directly toward where he thought his company would be. Riding closer would make him an excellent target as he topped rises; it was a whole lot safer to walk, at least until he could determine what he was up against.

The march to the first rise was incredibly hot. The water he had drunk at the water hole disappeared from his system in a matter of minutes, and he periodically sipped from the canteen he'd hung over his shoulder. When he was fifteen feet from the top of the rise, he dropped to the ground, crawled to its edge, and peered out.

What he saw was another, higher ridge.

He eased down into the broad pan between the ridges and trudged on, his senses as alert as they could be in the overpowering heat.

Lee had tired of the nagging "what if" images generated in her mind by the rider in the distance, so she hobbled Dancer and left him, walking toward the top of the gentle ridge that seemed to separate her from the stranger. The .38 hung in her right hand, with the hammer resting on an empty space in the cylinder. The climb to the top was deceptively steep. She crawled the last few feet to avoid placing her profile against the sky.

As she peeked over the ridge, she saw a man peek over another ridge. She flinched back immediately and saw the man do the same. When he levered a round into the chamber of his rifle, she drew back the hammer of her .38.

Then what she saw in front of her registered in her mind, and she began running, calling his name, covering the twenty yards between them at a speed that mocked the sun and the heat. She saw his shocked face light up with joy, and then he ran toward her too.

She launched herself at Ben, and he snatched her out of the air and swung her around, holding her close in an iron hug. She couldn't hold back tears of joy and relief when she felt his heart throbbing against her. They hugged desperately, thankfully, for a long, long moment. When they separated, they both began to speak at once. They laughed, paused, and did the same thing again. Finally Ben released his grip on her arms and stepped back.

"How in the world did you get here, Lee? How did you escape?" He stared into her eyes as she answered.

"I stole the best horse they had a couple days ago while the gang was having a powwow. They didn't bother to chase me much. I was just bait to Stone, anyway."

"Bait? I don't get it. How—"

"Stone has this crazy plan. He talked about it all the time. He wants to meet you in a saloon, just like the two of you did twenty years ago. He's insane—he's obsessed with gunning you down in a replica of where the first gunfight took place."

Ben shook his head. "We can talk about that later—but what about you? Are you all right? Did they hurt you? Did they . . . ?"

"I'm fine, Ben. Stone hit me a couple of times, but nothing else happened."

Ben's eyes narrowed, and a bit of the joy went out of them. He nodded without speaking, as if not trusting himself to say anything. "Where are they now?" he finally asked, his voice under control.

"I'm not sure. I overheard that they're going to cross over the Busted Backs, but that's all I know."

Ben glanced down at the pistol still clutched in Lee's hand. "Where'd you get that?"

"It was in the saddlebag of the horse I grabbed. I . . . I killed a rabbit with it. And I ate it."

He grinned at her. "Good for you. How'd you build your fire?"

"I didn't. I ate the meat raw."

He broke into laughter. "You're somethin', Lee," he chuckled. "And you did exactly the right thing. I got lucky. I picked up some lucifers, and I was able to—"

"Picked up? What do you mean?"

"Stone sent one of his men after me. There was a fight and . . . well, I killed him. I got some things out of his saddlebags, including the lucifers."

"Oh, Ben—I'm sorry." She could see the pain in his face. She'd seen it there before for the same reason, and now, just as she had previously, she tried to console him. "It's your job, Ben. It's unfortunate, but that doesn't make it any less true. You did what you had to do."

As she moved her head, her hair swung away from the blister on the side of her face. Ben stepped back.

"That's a burn, isn't it?"

"It doesn't bother me anymore. Don't worry about it."

He took some deep breaths and kept his eyes locked with hers, as if to keep them away from the mark on her face. When he spoke again, his voice was raspy. "They'll pay, Lee. I promise you that." He swallowed hard and changed the subject. "Where's this horse you stole?"

She pointed in the direction from which she'd come. "Back there a bit. He's a wonderful horse. Fast, bright, willing. You'll like him."

"I'm sure I will." He paused for a moment. "You think he can carry double for a little bit? I thought we'd go get him and ride him back to where I left Snorty."

"My Dancer could carry the state capitol building on his back if I asked him to. I'm not exaggerating about him. He's—"

"Dancer?"

"I named him Night Dancer when I was riding full tilt in the dark and he was dancing around rocks and scrub and prairie dog holes."

He laughed again. "Like I said, you're somethin', ma'am." He took her hand in his, and they began walking. After a short distance, he stopped abruptly and eased her into a gentle embrace. "I was real worried about you," he said, his voice husky with emotion.

"I was worried about you too. I prayed for you."

When they began walking again, Ben took her hand as he had earlier. Lee realized that they'd never held hands before. They didn't talk for a while. The silence felt good to her—as did the slight pressure between their hands.

Ben broke the silence after a few minutes. "Sam Turner was doing good when I left town. Doc worked on him. His arm's not gonna be right, but he'll live."

Lee looked more closely at him, extending gentle fingers to the wound on the side of his head. "Is this from the fight?" she asked quietly.

"Ain't much. It gave me some trouble at first, but it's better now." He whistled a long note as they topped the ridge beyond which Night Dancer was hobbled, his ears pointing at them with interest but not fear. "He's a looker, all right," Ben said. "His legs are straighter'n a ruler, and he's got a chest on him like a beer barrel. You got a good horse there."

Lee nodded. "But what's the legality? Can I keep him? I sure can't buy him from his owner—the man is dead.

Dancer was probably stolen, but finding his true owner would be just about impossible."

"No brand on him?"

"No. No marks at all."

"I'd say you got yourself a horse fair an' square. The way the law works is that any animal I end up with as a result of a felony being committed belongs to the town—and to me." He looked sideways at her. "Since I already own the finest piece of horse in Texas, I can't use your Dancer."

"I guess you forgot to add 'except for Slick' after the word Texas," she said in a teasing tone as she mounted the horse.

Ben smiled. "I didn't forget the words—it's just that I didn't need them."

He got up on the horse behind her, his hands resting on the rim of the cantle of her saddle. They rode for a while in silence.

"You still back there?" Lee finally asked. "You haven't said a word in forever."

Ben spoke after a moment, without the fun that'd been in her voice. "I'm still back here—and I don't figure on being much farther away from you than this for a while."

It was a good thing to say. Lee thought about it, about what it could mean.

"When we get back to Snorty," Ben continued, "we'll set up a little camp, and I'll go out on foot to see if I can find us some grub. I'd like you to have a good meal in you before you start back to Burnt Rock tomorrow. You won't make it in a day, but I'll give you my slicker to sleep under. You'll strike the town or tracks the next day for sure, and you'll sleep in your own bed that—"

"I'm not going back tomorrow," Lee interrupted. "I'm riding with you."

7

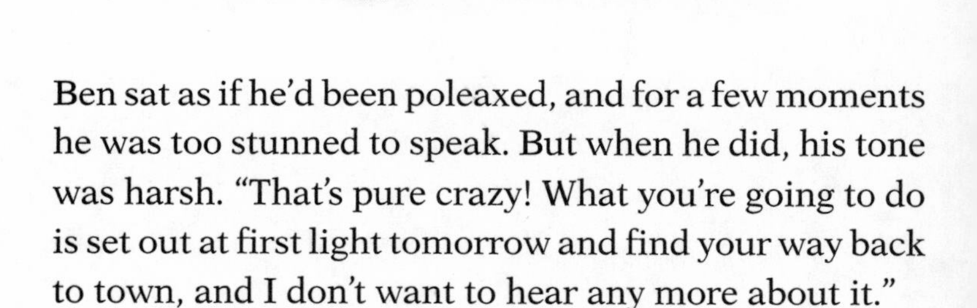

Ben sat as if he'd been poleaxed, and for a few moments he was too stunned to speak. But when he did, his tone was harsh. "That's pure crazy! What you're going to do is set out at first light tomorrow and find your way back to town, and I don't want to hear any more about it."

Lee reined in ten yards or so from where Snorty was ground tied. The horses glared at one another in the dimming light, neither willing to make the first overture toward acceptance. Ben slid off Dancer, and then Lee dismounted.

"Whether or not you want to hear about it, it's what's going to happen. I'm going on with you, and I'm going to help you put an end to the Stone gang."

"Absolutely not."

"Absolutely not?" she said, mocking his tone. "You sound like a schoolteacher telling a ten-year-old she can't bring her new puppy into the classroom! Who do you think you are to tell me I should run home because things might get sticky!"

"I know who I am. I'm the marshall of Burnt Rock, Texas. I'm in the course of my work, and I'm giving you a direct order. And I'll tell you something else: Things are going to get a lot more than sticky before this thing is finished."

"A direct order? What makes you think—"

"There's no reason for more arguing, Lee. You're heading for Burnt Rock tomorrow."

Her face was crimson with anger, and she swallowed a couple of times before speaking. "You chowderhead!" she snapped. "I thought at least you, of all the men in town, would have enough sense to realize that a woman is every bit as brave as a man, and every bit as ready to fight for what's right!"

"Look, the—"

"No, you look! You and every other cowpuncher and sodbuster in the West think women aren't good for anything but looking pretty and keeping quiet when the menfolk are talking. The whole silly bunch of you with your antiquated ideas are going to find out different real soon, Ben Flood! Women were already saving lives with the surgeons on the battlefields—Shiloh, Gettysburg, Antietam—and now back East we're being recognized as real people who can accomplish as much as a man. Why—"

"All I said was that you aren't going to get caught up between me an' a bunch of desperados who've already proved they'd just as soon kill as not! 'Course women deserve better'n they get. My point is that you don't have the skills to be of any help to me."

Her voice was suddenly arctic; icicles seemed to hang from each word. "What skills are you referring to?"

He spoke before thinking. "Shooting and riding and being able to—"

"You, sir, are terribly mistaken!" she shrieked. "On the worst day I ever had, I could outride you! And do you think the rabbit I ate *volunteered* to become food? I got it with a pistol that's probably twenty years old and that I'd never even tried before I had to fire it!"

"There's a lotta difference between dropping a rabbit and killing a man. For one thing, the rabbit doesn't have a Sharp's and a skinful of Mexican liquor, an' isn't out lookin' to spill your blood."

"Don't patronize me, Ben. I know the dangers. I was with Stone, remember? I realize that I'm not a gunfighter. In fact, I'd never pointed a weapon at a living thing until I killed that first rabbit. But that doesn't change anything. I have the skills to help you. I think you'd better start figuring out that you *do* need me."

He threw up his hands in exasperation, then spun on his heel and stalked over to where Snorty stood still glaring at Dancer. "I'm going to get us some food," he snarled over his shoulder. "If you're such a top hand with horses, how about getting these two together without them chewin' an' kickin' pieces outta each other?" He tugged the rifle from his saddle scabbard and set off on foot toward a small rise that was still visible in the dusk. He saw that he had maybe an hour or slightly longer to shoot whatever he could and get it back to camp.

As he trudged away, he felt confused by the sensation he was experiencing. What was it? Was it anger that caused him to clench his left fist so tightly that his fingernails were digging into his palm? He didn't know. But what he did know was that what he'd felt for Lee not fifteen minutes ago was real, a powerful surge of emotion he'd never experienced before. When he'd first seen her as they topped the ridge and their eyes met, it was as if a terrible pain in his heart had suddenly eased, as if dark night had turned to bright day. But now . . .

What she proposed was nonsense! She knew nothing of the terror that accompanied any fight to the death. She rode wonderfully, and her skills on horseback were strong. He'd seen her perform the flying mount, the switch from horse to horse at a full gallop, the barebacked jumping over a parked delivery wagon loaded with two layers of sacks of grain. And he'd seen her groundwork; he'd watched her gentle a mare after a fight with another mare that left both horses bleeding and ready to continue the battle, and he'd watched, awed, as she rode an aggressive stallion to a standstill after the horse had done his level best to throw her over the moon. *But none of that was done with lead in the air or rifle sights looking for her heart or her back!*

Or was it? She'd snatched a horse out of the middle of Stone's gang and lived to tell about it.

Suddenly a fat jackrabbit squirted out from behind some scrub a few feet from him and was just as quickly swallowed up by a patch of mesquite. He hadn't even gotten the rifle off his shoulder. He berated himself for letting his thoughts carry him away.

He looked down at his rifle. He knew Lee had a good eye with weapons. She'd looked at three new rifles the town had purchased for his office to arm posse members, should he need to assemble one in a hurry, and she'd handled the long guns with respect but not fear. After twenty minutes she was shooting a cluster of six rounds into a pie-plate-sized target at forty yards. She was handy with a pistol too. They'd dragged out into the prairie a sack of empty syrup bottles from O'Keefe's Café, and Lee shattered her targets cleanly and quickly, shooting six times and breaking the last bottle while the shards of the first two were still in the air.

But targets and bottles don't shoot back.

When Ben strode back into camp, the light of day was almost gone. He threw together a fire and got it going before skinning the rabbit, two blacksnakes, and a prairie hen he'd killed. Lee had Dancer and Snorty grazing together in the same stretch of dry grass. He grinned. No one would ever suspect the two of being friends, but they tolerated one another without open warfare.

Ben put the meat on the spit and the peach can full of water on the fire to boil. Then he squatted down and turned the meat over the flames. He looked over at Lee.

They hadn't really spoken since he'd returned with the game.

He caught her eye, and she moved forward and put her hand lightly on his shoulder. His throat constricted with emotion; she had never looked so beautiful to him. The light from the flames flickered across her face, lining her sculpted cheekbones in brass and imbuing her hair with an inner light that gave it the hue of a melted black diamond. Her eyes were incandescent, and their chestnut glow, fragmented by the flames, turned to sparks of copper and black.

She moved over to sit next to him. "I've seen how Stone operates," she said. "I don't know much about a person being possessed by an evil spirit, but I do know that he is. He's so cold. Life means nothing to him. Maybe the only thing that does mean anything to him is killing you, Ben."

"Maybe so. But none of that means it's your fight. I'm a marshall. I enforce the law. Some days Nick and I play checkers and drink coffee, an' other days we risk our lives. That's the job."

"The job is going against a mad-dog killer and ten other men alone?"

"If that's what it takes. I couldn't leave the town with no lawman, and I couldn't ask a civilian to get involved in this thing."

A bit of exasperation crept back into Lee's voice. "Couldn't you at least wire for some help, then?"

"Don't need it."

"You *do* need it—and I can give it to you! Look, I'm not planning to ride into Stone's camp shooting, but I can create a diversion, free the horses, confuse those killers while you do what you have to do." She stood. "Think about it," she said as she walked off into the darkness, her tall form silhouetted momentarily as the cloud cover broke in front of the moon.

Ben sighed and poured the last of his coffee beans into the peach can. Then he began to pray for guidance. What she said made some sense, in a way . . .

Their meal was quiet but not uneasy. Lee ate the meat from the blade of her knife; Ben ate his directly from the stick he'd cooked it on. The roasted food tasted as good as anything she'd ever eaten. As she helped herself to some more snake, she caught Ben grinning at her.

"What?"

"I've never known a woman other than my ma who'd eat snake, till I met you. It shows some grit."

She shrugged. "Food's food. Have you thought over what I said?"

He prodded and dragged the can of coffee off the embers with his stick and left it to cool a foot from the fire. "Yeah. I have. I can use you, but the idea scares me. We'd need some ground rules if we're goin' to ride together."

"Like what?"

Ben counted them off on the fingers of his right hand. "We never go in together. Your work will be kinda behind the scenes, like you said. You don't expose yourself to gunfire if you can avoid it—and that means you turn tail rather than face guns, no matter what's going on." He paused.

"Go on," she urged.

"Here's the most important one: If something happens to me—if I get shot or captured or whatever—you head for home, an' by home, I mean Burnt Rock. I need your word on that, an' I'll ask you to swear on my Bible to make sure I've got it."

"What if I could get you out somehow? What if—"

"I ain't about to negotiate on this, Lee. That's the way it's gonna be, or I'm goin' on alone."

"I'd follow you if you tried that."

Ben sighed. "I'll tell you what. If it comes down to it, I'll tie you over your saddle like a sack of grain, carry you back to town, lock you up, an' set off again, on my own. Nick'd let you out in a few days. I'd lose some time doin' all that, but I'd do it."

A long moment passed. Finally she spoke. "Yes. I'm sure you would. Fetch your Bible."

The oath he asked her to repeat with her hand resting on the cover of his Bible was a simple one, short and succinct, the crux of it being that she would immediately ride to Burnt Rock rather than attempt to help him if he were captured. If he were wounded but able to make it to their camp, it would be him who decided if she stayed or rode off for help. If he were killed, she'd head for town.

Ben set his Bible aside and picked up the can. He passed it to Lee, and she took a long drink. The brew was strong enough to melt a horseshoe. The *ahhh* she released after swallowing brought a smile to his face.

"I've yet to see anyone—man or woman—who enjoys a cup of coffee as much as you do. You'd think it was milk an' honey the way you drink it down."

She returned the smile. "This beat-up tin can is a far cry from a cup, but you're right. The blacker and stronger it is, the better I like it." She handed the can to Ben, and he lowered its level by half before handing it back.

"I need to know what you're planning," she said after sipping at the coffee again.

"There's not much to it, really. We'll ride by day till we catch up with Stone and then do all our work at night. They're a squirrelly enough bunch to begin with, and I can't see the gang holdin' together if members start gettin' killed or captured. I think we can play on their weakness—kinda turn them against one another. Once we start our attacks, we're gonna keep right at it, hittin' them every night, till they're afraid to sleep an' too mad to shoot or think straight. Stone's the craziest of the group. He might even break first an' do something stupid that'd let me take him."

Lee swallowed some more coffee. "I wouldn't bet on that. You're right, he's crazy, but he's . . . well . . . he knows what he's doing too, I guess. Killing you in a gunfight is more important to him than anything else in his life, and the hold evil has on him is so strong that he'll hold himself together until he gets what he wants, or is captured, or . . . or killed."

"You don't like to use that word, do you? I don't particularly either. But you got to recognize that's most likely the way this thing will play out. Stone won't give up, and he won't go in alive."

Lee hesitated a moment. "Are you better than Zeb Stone?"

"Yeah. But that doesn't mean much. Gunfights aren't like horse races, where the fastest and the strongest almost always wins. If it comes to me an' Stone facin' one another, it's anybody's bet who walks away. If he put notches in his gun, he'd have whittled away the grips by now. He's been in lots more face-to-face gunfights than I have, and he knows all the tricks there are to know."

"You know something more important than a gunman's tricks, Ben. You know God. That's what counts."

Ben nodded in agreement. "Back in town, Stone said I was nothin' without my voodoo book. I told him he was right." He stood and stretched his back. "I'd like to get moving with first light tomorrow an' cover some ground before the heat gets bad."

He walked toward where the horses grazed. In a moment, Lee joined him. Snorty and Dancer were separated by fifteen feet or so and seemed to want to keep that distance. Ben stood next to Dancer, stroking his neck.

"Muscles on this boy like they're cut out of spring steel," he commented. He carried their saddles closer to the fire, took his own rifle, and handed it to Lee. "You keep this handy from now on," he said. "I've got all the ammo we need, an' I'll split it up between our saddlebags tomorrow." He spread his slicker on one side of the fire and Snorty's saddle blanket on the other.

"Well," he said. "Good night."

Lee hid her smile; the light from the fire had shown her the blush on his face. "Good night," she said and settled down on the slicker, rolling over once to bring it close around her body.

The sound of gunfire ahead—first, a spatter of pistol rounds that sounded like the pops of cheap firecrackers, and then a burst of deeper, louder rifle fire that went on for half a minute—brought a wide grin to Zeb Stone's face. He reined in and held up his hand to stop the others, then waved them toward him.

"Some of you boys thought I was turnin' yellow, not takin' the fast ride over the Busted Backs. Well, I'll tell you what: Them gunshots mean only one thing—that takin' the route the traders an' drummers use makes nothin' but good sense. The men I sent ahead ain't shootin' at targets. I don't know what they're onto, but somethin's ours that weren't ours before. Lissen up, now."

The group sat on their horses quietly for a long moment. There were no more shots.

"Good. The fightin's over."

The conversations burst forth around him, focused on what the scouts had come across, each outlaw hoping something of value waited for them a few miles ahead: whiskey, horses, women, money, cattle, firearms—the things that made life worthwhile.

Stone held the men back from beating their horses into a mad gallop. "Whatever it is, it ain't goin' nowhere," he shouted. "First man to break away gets a slug from my Sharp's in his back. I want these horses kept alive!"

He lit a cigar, slowly rolling its head in the flame of the match, purposely taunting his followers. He looked from man to man, and not one made eye contact. That made him feel powerful, better than this group of gunslingers and crazies who wouldn't live a month without him to lead them. Those the bounty hunters and the law didn't get would kill one another in stupid fights over nothing. The thought brought a grin to his face as he nudged his horse into a walk.

Ahead was a gentle curve to the left that swung around a knoll covered with brown grass. Stone used his heels to goad his horse into a lope, and the others followed, most of them whooping and hollering in anticipation. The scene opened up to them as soon as they rounded the bend. The body of a young man—a hired hand or a drifter from the looks of his worn and disheveled clothing—rested on its side in the rutted dirt of the path. Twenty feet beyond the young fellow was another body, that of an old man whose white hair spread around his head in the dirt like a halo. A wagon with a pair of mules in the traces was angled into the scrub grass near the corpse.

One of Stone's scouts was sitting on the edge of the wagon, head tilted far backward and a bottle to his lips. The other scout was pawing through the small wooden crates stacked two high on the wagon, tossing what were apparently women's dresses over his shoulder. The clothes fluttered to the ground like wounded butterflies, the colors bright against the drab earth tones of the prairie.

Stone held up his hand with the cigar between his fingers to stop the men behind him and rode up to the wagon. "Whadda we got here?"

The drinker lowered his bottle. "An ol' drummer an' his helper, looks like. Me an' Tory, we found a case of booze an' a bunch of clothes so far, but we ain't gone through but a few of the crates."

"Any money?"

"None I seen, but we ain't found their personal stuff yet. This is a pretty fair load of merchandise. They might have some money or gold hid out."

Stone took a drag from his cigar and tossed the last inch or so to the side. He exhaled a stream of smoke and then raised his arm to wave the rest of the gang forward.

The outlaws came on like a wave, skinning down from their horses and clambering over the wagon, punching and kicking their mates away from the crates, cursing, shouting, claiming goods they couldn't yet see as they used their saddle or sheath knives to force open the wooden boxes. Several of them grabbed bottles of whiskey from the already-opened case. Dishes—saucers, plates, a serving platter—sailed into the air, where they were shattered by an elongated burst of gunfire. An outlaw kicked a case of lanterns off the edge of the wagon, and the crash of breaking glass was overcome by the melee.

The mules, wide-eyed and almost petrified with fear, stood rigid and unmoving, the hide over their backs twitching frantically. A crate of hammers joined the lanterns on the ground next to the wagon, and a cheer went up as another case of whiskey was found. Several outlaws fought viciously over a crate of boots, although there were more pairs than desperadoes.

Stone stepped from his saddle to the wagon and grabbed the two nearest men. "Git them mules unhitched an' tie 'em off by them trees. Make sure they don' git away—we can use 'em." He shoved a man pawing at the second case of whiskey and tossed a bottle to each of the outlaws he'd ordered to secure the mules. The hardness left their faces and their eyes, and they stopped to pull corks and dump liquor down their throats before hustling the mules away from the frenzy.

Ladies' corsets filled the air for a moment and were almost immediately replaced by a flurry of camisoles and bloomers. Axes and hatchets bound together with heavy wire in bundles of ten were shoved to the ground, where the heads clanged together almost musically.

Stone swung onto his horse's back and rode a few yards away from the wagon, watching. He'd seen timber wolves tearing the life out of an aged moose chased into exhaustion when he'd been on the run in Canada; watching his men now was almost as much fun. He kicked his boots out of the stirrups and lit another cigar. Up ahead where the boys were tying the mules was as good a place as any to make camp for the night.

All in all, it hadn't been a bad haul. The drummers were carrying mostly dry goods and tools and other worthless weight, but the cases of whiskey had been a good find. And there'd been a thousand rounds of .45 caliber bullets that'd been manufactured by Remington, which meant the bullets would fire properly, unlike the army junk that presented a crapshoot each time the trigger was pulled. The boots were Mexican made and looked to be of decent quality; those who weren't too drunk to do so hauled off their old boots and replaced them with the new. And several outlaws now had turnip-shaped pocket watches on silver chains, which were as useless as the ladies' bloomers to them, since only Stone and one other man knew how to set or read a watch.

The drummers hadn't had much money with them; the freight they were hauling most likely represented C.O.D. contracts. Stone found a good pair of spurs in a carpetbag hidden under the board seat of the wagon, along with a framed daguerreotype of a hefty, plain-faced woman standing stiffly and staring grimly at the camera, with her hands on the shoulders of a young boy. He casually tossed the picture aside. He was about to discard the bag too when he felt the weight of something he'd missed at its bottom. Reaching in, he pulled out a small, well-used Bible. His face wrinkled in disgust. He was about to throw the book into the scrub when he got a better idea—a much better idea. He slipped the book into his saddlebag.

The wagon and mules would come in handy. And they'd found a case of five-pound cans of Armor's potted meat, so they'd eat well for a while. He watched as his men set fire to sheaves of sheet music and several pounds of novels.

It had been a very good day.

The two horses glared at one another, their movements jerky, almost wooden, sweat gleaming on the rigid muscles of their chests. Ben gave Snorty the slightest bit of rein to ease him out of a walk. The horse got under the mild bit and launched himself forward as if he'd been fired from a powerful catapult.

Dancer jammed ahead in response, his rear hooves scattering dirt and pebbles as he wrestled with Lee's firm hands on the reins. She gave him his head for a heartbeat, but at the same time used the hackamore to bring him around in a wide circle, ending up a few feet to the right of Ben and Snorty—the same place she'd started from.

"I always enjoy an early morning ride on a well-behaved mount," she said, her brow showing sweat although they'd been in the saddle less than five minutes.

"You're the one with patience with horses," Ben said. "My idea is to take these two bangtails and slam their silly heads together till they listen to reason."

"Patience? Right this minute, I've got about as much patience as a scorpion in a frying pan." She pushed back with her forearm the hair glued by sweat to her forehead. "Let's see if I can follow you. Go on ahead—I'll let you gain ten yards or so on me and see what happens."

Ben tapped his heels against Snorty's barrel. Snorty wrenched his head and showed his teeth to Dancer, and then he stepped ahead very reluctantly, his tail beginning to revolve like the blades on a windmill. Ben was turning his body to speak to Lee when she and Dancer wheeled past him, moving clumsily sideways, rising a cloud of dust. Before Ben could tighten his own reins, Snorty stretched his neck and tore a mouthful of hide out of Dancer's flank, leaving a bare and bloody wound the size of a man's palm.

Dancer tried to rear, even though Lee had his head almost welded to his own left side and the reins in a death grip in her hands. The awkward and unbalanced position seemed to have no effect on Dancer—he spun as close to a gallop as a bent-in-half horse could do. Lee's face was crimson, although the color was difficult to see, since all the dust she and her horse had put into the air seemed to be adhering to her face.

She wrapped the left rein around the saddle horn to hold Dancer's head in place. Standing in the stirrups, she leaned far forward and took the horse's right ear in her mouth. Then she bit down hard. Dancer stopped quickly, as if he had run into a stone wall, and stood with frantic eyes. His breath came out in rasps and a squeal of pain formed in his throat. Lee let off the pressure, and when Dancer once again began to spin, she chewed down on his ear, stopping him so quickly that he stumbled over himself and came close to going down.

Ben watched the scene before him. He kept a tight hold on Snorty, which was difficult to do, not because Snorty was acting up, but because he himself was laughing so hard.

Lee again eased the pressure of her teeth off Dancer's ear. He began to spin, but his movements were now unsure and much slower than they had been before. She grabbed his ear between her teeth for the third time, and the horse stopped. And again, she released her teeth. This time, Dancer stood still, his eyes as wide as wagon wheels. He shook his head, and she unwrapped the rein from her saddle horn and cued the horse to walk. Dancer did so, and Ben watched incredulously as the tension left the animal and his muscles returned to their normal state.

Ben jogged Snorty up beside Lee and wasn't surprised to see him settle down and lose interest in battling with Dancer. Ben knew it took two to make a fight or a race, and if one of the parties wasn't interested, there was no dispute. Just like the previous night; if Snorty and Dancer didn't infringe upon one another, they got along just fine.

Lee daintily turned her head away from Ben as she picked horsehairs from her lips and off her tongue. When she turned back, she said quite seriously, "I hope you were paying attention, because if you don't behave, I'll do the same thing to you."

Ben couldn't laugh anymore. He wiped the tears from his eyes and face with his sleeve and gasped for breath. "You're most definitely a horse corrector, Miss Morgan," he said. "I've seen a few men who'll grab an ear in their fist when they're ridin' down a real rank horse, but I never saw anyone bite an ear before."

"I wasn't just biting. I was blowing air into his ear too. I've won more than a minor skirmish here. Dancer knows I can do it again."

"'Deed he does. You know, I was thinkin' we should let them run it out—see who was the fastest, tire them out a bit, and then look for some cooperation after we got their edges off. Your way worked better. Dancer might not have taken well to bein' dusted by Snorty. A good horse can lose his spirit when—"

"Ben, there's more bottom in this horse than you've ever dreamed of. Early speed doesn't make a good mount. It's how he behaves after eighteen hours under saddle, picking strays out of brambles . . . or . . ."

Ben smiled at her. "I guess we'll find out one day, won't we?"

She responded to his supercilious smile with one of her own. "We sure will find out." She cued Dancer into a gentle lope. Ben and Snorty stayed at her side, and the horses moved in unison, covering ground with so little effort that it seemed they could hold the lope for the rest of the day without slowing.

As they rode toward the Busted Backs, the mountains seemed bizarrely elusive. It seemed that each stride the horses took pushed the shambling group of foothills farther away. When they stopped midday to share a canteen of water and to fill Ben's Stetson for each of the horses, Lee dismounted and stretched her back. Then she cocked her hand over her eyes like a visor and said, "It looks like there's a lake up ahead. Is there? With all the shimmering from the heat, it's hard to tell, but it sure looks like water."

"There's no water and no lake, Lee. That's a mirage and nothin' but a mirage." He wiped his sleeve across his face and caught the quick look of dejection on her face. "Don't let it get to you. We're doin' fine, eating miles and making good time. The thing is, the way things look get all fouled up out here in this heat. It can cause a person to see things that aren't there, and particularly things he or she most wants to see—like the lake that's teasin' you." He wiped his face again. "We'll stop for a bit at the first water hole we come to, and in another few hours I'll start watchin' for our supper."

"I'd give anything to wash out these clothes I'm wearing," Lee sighed. "And I'm as grubby as a saloon floor myself. I must smell like a month's hard labor."

He grinned at her. "Neither one of us are what you'd call a fresh rose right now. I'm right sure we'll cut a stream a few miles into the Backs. It's probably not runnin' real hard right now, but it's runnin', an' we'll be able to wash our clothes and ourselves in it."

"That sounds wonderful. Let's keep moving. I want to make sure you're not wrong, and that *is* a lake up ahead."

8

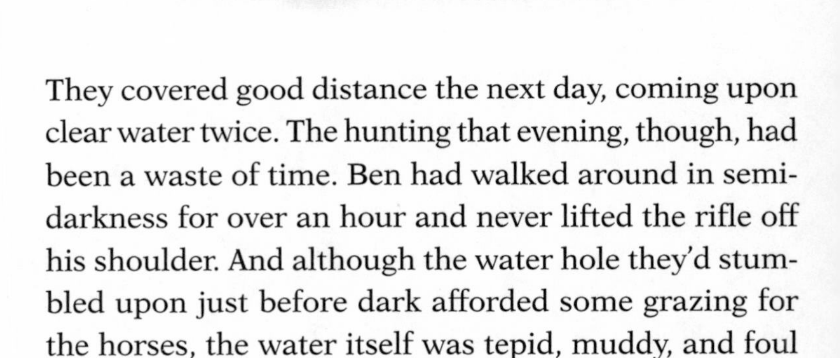

They covered good distance the next day, coming upon clear water twice. The hunting that evening, though, had been a waste of time. Ben had walked around in semi-darkness for over an hour and never lifted the rifle off his shoulder. And although the water hole they'd stumbled upon just before dark afforded some grazing for the horses, the water itself was tepid, muddy, and foul tasting.

Ben built a fire and fueled it with mesquite branches, but the smoke did little but remind the two of them how hungry they were. They prayed together aloud and then individually as they settled in for the night on opposite sides of the fire. The day's ride under the unrelenting sun had pushed them both to the edge of exhaustion.

Coyotes woke Ben.

He checked the position of the moon without moving, noting that the night was approaching its end. There was a vague line of soft yellow-red light at the eastern horizon, but the prairie was still dark. When the coyote bayed again, Ben scanned the hills, seeking it out. He was surprised—and thankful—when he located it about seventy-five yards away, on a small knoll that defined the animal's lean body against the horizon. Ben's rifle was next to him, just outside the saddle blanket he'd wrapped around himself. He eyed the coyote again.

Probably closer to a hundred yards than seventy-five, he thought. *Coyote ain't much for flavor. Meat's bound to be stringy and overly lean, an' we got nothin' to put on it to make it taste better. Will Lee eat it?* He smiled. He knew the answer to that question. He listened to her breathing for several moments, gauging the depth of her sleep. A blast from the 30.30 would wake her in a big hurry. *Can't be helped.*

He eased his hand out from under the saddle blanket and touched the cold barrel of the rifle. He'd have to sit up and bring the stock to his shoulder in a single motion. His body position was good; the coyote would appear in the front sight with very little movement on his part. He'd jacked a round into place the night before, so he didn't need to cock the rifle.

Ben knew that coyotes stay alive by being skittish; any metallic sound screamed "man" at them. But he felt no wind, no breeze, on the skin of his face. The shot would be dead-on. He moved his hand down the barrel toward the stock as carefully as if he were stroking a feverish infant.

"What are you doing?"

The whisper was so quiet that Ben wondered if it was a thought rather than a sound until he looked at Lee and saw her opened eyes. A tiny bit of reflected moonlight caught on something metal, and he squinted toward her. The damaged pistol was curled in her hand, its muzzle pointed upward. He moved his head an inch to either side to indicate there was no danger and shifted his concentration back to the coyote.

The animal's head was coming up, and a howl was beginning to resonate from deep within its chest. Ben fit his hand to the action of the 30.30 and sat up, the saddle blanket falling to his lap from his upper body. He brought the rifle to his shoulder rapidly but smoothly, leaning his cheek against the cold wood. The sight slid effortlessly through the chill air to the point where it stopped on the juncture of the coyote's chest and neck. Ben held a shallow breath and eased the trigger back. He'd been ready for the thunderous report and so had Lee, but they both flinched at the deep-throated blast. The coyote appeared to leap straight up at the sky, then it fell to its side and was still. The echo from the shot reverberated in the hills around them, dying slowly.

Ben stood and ratcheted out the empty cartridge. "He's down for good," he said. "See if you can get any life out of the fire. I'll skin the coyote and be back with the meat.

It'll probably be like eating a tin roof, but it'll stick with us. We got a hard day coming up."

Lee stood and stretched. "Nice shot. I've never eaten coyote. Have you?"

"Yeah," he said, laughing. "The last time I had dinner with the Queen of England. She's real partial to it."

Lee grinned as she poked at the fire with a length of mesquite and found live embers below the surface of burned-out coals. "If it's good enough for the Queen, it's good enough for me."

There was an otherworldly texture to everything around Ben as he walked to the knoll where the coyote lay. The silence wrapped itself around him like a shroud, and although he knew there was abundant life around and even under the prairie, he could hear nothing. It was the sort of silence he imagined would exist on the moon.

As it always did in the moments before dawn, the narrow strand of new light at the horizon promised a new day, a good day. Ben stopped for a moment and watched as the pastels began to harden into brighter, more vivid colors and the shadows lost their sharp edges and began to creep back to the objects that cast them.

He hunkered down next to the dead coyote with his boot knife in his hand, its blade sharper than that of a straight razor. The process didn't take long.

The fire was burning nicely when Ben carried the meat back to their camp. He found Lee leading Snorty away from the water hole. "Neither one of them drank much," she said. "They're leery about the taste. They'll need a long drink of the first sweet water we cross."

"This stuff tastes like it ran off a saloon floor, but there's lots of small streams and spring-fed water holes ahead. There'll be plenty of good water." He speared the thin slabs of red meat on a mesquite branch and held it over the flames. In a moment, what little fat there was began to drip, and the fire grew, reaching toward the skewered meat as if claiming it.

"Smells pretty good," Lee observed.

The coyote did smell good; the smoke that surrounded the campfire brought saliva to his mouth.

"Can we take any of the meat with us?"

He shook his head. "I wish we could—but we can't. Even after a single day in the heat, it'll be unfit to eat." He rotated the stick slowly, checking the meat. "Looks like it's about as done as it'll ever be. Ready?"

The coyote meat had the texture of scorched rope and was sharp tasting, as if it had been marinated in lamp fuel. Neither Ben nor Lee commented on the flavor. "Like you said the other day," Ben finally offered, "food is food."

The climb was gradual through most of the morning. Soon, however, when the sun was at its highest, the ground seemed to tilt sharply upward, presenting faces that were bare of any growth and littered with rocks and loose stones.

The slanting, baking walls looked as upright as the side of a good barn and seemed to stretch toward the sky for miles. Lee knew Snorty was a good climber and that he used his muscles and the weight of his body athletically, gaining the most ground with the least possible expenditure of energy.

Dancer was another story. He broke a nervous sweat as she guided him up the first climb. His eyes grew wide as he struggled upward, and his hide seemed tense enough to strike a match on. When his breathing grew raspy and hoarse—from fear rather than exertion—Lee reined in at the face of a long climb and dismounted.

Ben stopped next to her as she checked her girth and the set of the hackamore. "Trouble?"

"Nothing I can't handle," she answered. "I don't want to goad him, but I can't afford to spend the day arguing with him at the base of each slope either." She stepped ahead and ran her hand the length of Dancer's sweaty neck. "He's just scared is all. He's one of the most agile and quick-footed horses I've ever ridden, but he doesn't know that yet." She shook Dancer's sweat off her hand. "His heart's beating way too fast. He'll run himself into the ground before we're halfway to the other side."

Ben stepped down and stood next to her. "If we can get him up an' over a couple of climbs, he'll be fine. Be good if we could rope him to Snorty, but that won't work—they're still sorting things out between them, an' a ruckus on a slope could hurt either or both of them real bad."

"You're right—that's too dangerous." Lee wiped the sweat from her forehead. "We might just as well water them here. I need a couple of minutes to think this over. I know Dancer can top these climbs, but I've got to get him to realize that too."

Dancer didn't completely refuse a climb until later that afternoon. The face was a long one, steep and treacherous because of its composition of flint and shale. The horse wheeled, flinging long strands of spittle from his gaping mouth. His muscles were so tight that they trembled under his sweat-drenched skin, and his breathing sounded like a rasp being dragged across rusted steel.

Ben eased Snorty past Lee and Dancer. "I'll take it first, and maybe he'll follow."

"No—just give me some room. I'm going up this climb on my horse one way or another." She gave Dancer some rein and let him scramble a few yards away from the slope. She pointed him at it and sat still in her saddle, letting the horse eye the stone face as long as he cared to. *Come on, Dancer. You can do it.*

The horse walked toward the climb when she cued him to do so. She reined him in and sat quietly in the saddle. Then she took a couple of deep breaths and opened her mouth wide.

Her scream was so loud, so piercing, and so unexpected that Dancer forgot about his fear. Lee knew that his instinct and his heart were telling him to get away from the banshee that was attacking him. He charged ahead in panic, putting a storm of grit and stone in the air as he fought for traction.

At the top, he hung his head for a couple of minutes, gulping air. When he raised his head and turned back to look at Lee, the lack of white around his eyes told her the fear was gone. She stroked his neck.

"Good boy, Dancer," she murmured. Then she hollered down to Ben. "Come on! You're wasting time!"

They stayed in the saddle for the rest of the day, stopped at a water hole at dusk, and decided to ride into the night, since the sky was so clear and the moon was offering good light. They camped well after midnight in a narrow little valley between two buttes. There was no need for a fire; they'd crossed no game during the long day. But there was good grazing for the horses and sweet water in the valley.

The next morning, Lee awakened to someone gently shaking her shoulder.

"I think we're gettin' close, Lee," Ben was saying. "I want to head out as soon as you're ready."

She rolled out of the slicker, stretched like a cat, and smiled. *Not a bad way to be awakened,* she thought.

It was late afternoon when they struck the stream Ben had mentioned the day before. It was shallow but running well, and a small copse of trees and grass made the scene idyllic. They loosened their saddles and let the horses drink their fill before turning them out into the grass. Lee attached the hobbles to Dancer's forelegs but allowed him so much slack that he could almost gallop if he'd wanted to. The horses grazed happily, maintaining enough space between them so that neither felt threatened. Lee told Ben that she planned to be rid of the hobbles when they rode out. Dancer showed no interest in leaving her. After seeing to the horses, she filled the canteens at the edge of the stream and then pulled off her battered shoes, groaning with the pleasure of it.

"What I'd like you to do is go out and shoot something to eat, Ben. Call out before you ride back in, because I'm going to take a bath, and I don't want to be surprised." She thought for a moment. "I'll tell you something: I can't stand these clothes another minute. I'm going to wash them too. Why don't you go ahead and take a bath yourself and shoot our supper, and I'll join you when my clothes are dry enough to put back on. That shouldn't be long, even with the sun starting to set. OK?"

"Suits me fine. I'll follow the stream for a bit till I find a good site and set up a fire. Then I'll take a bath an' let my clothes dry right on me. I should have something to cook before you catch up." He took his backup Colt from his saddlebag and handed it, grips first, to Lee. "I'm worried about that piece of junk you're carryin'. You got lucky with it, but chances are it'll blow up in your face if you pull the trigger again. I'd like you to pitch it an' keep this one with you."

She reached out and accepted the pistol. "Are you going to be all right without this? Won't you feel kind of . . . well . . . naked without it?"

Ben's smile was wide. "If it came to a time when I needed that gun, I probably couldn't get to it fast enough to save my hide. My second gun is nothing but insurance, and poor insurance at that. We'll transfer some bullets from my saddlebag to yours later on."

"Thanks, Ben." She hefted the pistol, feeling the weight of it. It fit her hand well. She rolled out the cylinder to check the load. "This isn't going to do me any good if I don't know how it handles."

He nodded. "Go right ahead an' run some rounds through it. The pistol's dead-on up to about thirty feet; then it tends to the left a little. You've got a good eye—you'll figure it out."

He tugged a dozen or so cartridges from the loops in his gun belt and handed them to Lee, who dropped them into her pocket. She held back one, which she inserted into the empty space under the hammer. The other five spaces already contained bullets.

She looked over at him. "What about the noise? If we're close to Stone, he's bound to hear the shots."

"Don't make any difference now. He knows I'm comin' on after him. What he doesn't know is when I'll hit him. Go ahead an' shoot."

Lee glanced over to where the horses were grazing and then turned to the open prairie. The weight of the .45 caused her to hold her right wrist with her left hand, not in a death lock, but more as a support. As she lifted the pistol chest high, she extended it at arm's length and swung it an arc in front of her, finger outside of the trigger guard.

"That rock there by the tumbleweed is about twenty feet out," Ben said, standing a couple of feet behind her. "Give it a try at that range."

She eased her left foot back a bit, aligning her body with the target. Then she squeezed off a round that dug a rut in the sandy soil a couple of inches to the left of her target. After lowering the pistol, she paused for a moment, raised it, and fired again. The first shot launched the rock a yard into the air. She glanced at the horses, who were watching but not overly concerned. When the rock landed, her third and fourth rounds skittered it along the ground several feet. The fifth shattered it, putting a cloud of brown grit and shards of stone into the air. Her sixth shot clipped a small piece broken from the original target and sent it spinning off to one side.

"Good shootin'," Ben said. *Good? It was terrific shootin'!* "Try something farther out."

Lee loaded the cylinder, closed it, and scanned the ground beyond the shattered rock. A small saguaro cactus thirty-five feet away caught her eye. She fast-fired this time, squeezing the trigger smoothly but quickly. The first round whined past the cactus; the second exploded the ground a foot in front of it. The last four shots shredded the plant, scattering the pulpy whiteness of its core in all directions. She lowered the pistol to reload.

"It's a real fine weapon, Ben. Thanks again." She closed the cylinder. "Now, how about going down the stream so a lady can have a bath?"

"Sure." He turned away before she could see the awed smile on his face. *The lady shoots like John Wesley Hardin,* he thought. *She's a Christian, she eats snake an' coyote without a word, and she cares enough about me to risk her life*. For the first time in many years, Ben found himself whistling as he walked along.

Lee found a small pool the size of a large tabletop and about three feet deep. The water was clear, and the bottom was sandy. She undressed quickly and settled into the pool, sighing with pleasure. The water was colder than she thought it would be, but that made no difference. She leaned forward, submerged her head, and rubbed vigorously at the dirt and sweat that had accumulated in her hair. When she came up for air, she spewed water from her mouth like a fountain. She scoured her body with handfuls of sand until her skin felt fresh and a whole lot cleaner. Finally, she rubbed at her hair again until it squeaked under her kneading fingers. She left the pool for a moment, padded to where she'd left her clothing, carried it to the pool, and lowered herself back in.

The current had returned the water to its original crystal clarity in the short time she'd been out of it. She scrubbed her clothes with sand and rinsed everything thoroughly. As she worked on her skirt, her fingers touched a hard lump in a pocket. She found the lump again and pulled out the piece of blade-shaped stone she'd picked up when she was a captive. She returned it to the pocket. Finally, she laid out everything on the ground to dry.

Her body dried quickly, even though the sun was beginning to relinquish its power for the day. When her clothes had dried enough to be considered only damp, she dressed.

Ben picked off a pair of rabbits with an equal number of shots as he followed the stream away from Lee. About a mile from where he'd left her, he came upon a campsite that looked good; the stream, swift but shallow here, offered all the water they could use, and there was some patchy grass for grazing. Mesquite trees grew close together in a ragged jumble of limbs and branches a few yards from the stream. He tugged off dead branches and gathered those already on the ground and stacked them as neatly as he could, creating a broad-based campfire that would burn all night. Without lighting the fire, he ground tied Snorty and walked farther along the stream until he came to a section that seemed deeper. He wrestled his boots off on the shore, took off his vest and gun belt, emptied his pockets, and tiptoed into the water.

The water was chilly but not actually cold; it felt good as it soaked him to the waist. He held his Stetson under the water, wrung it out, and repeated the operation before tossing the hat back toward his boots and gun. When he crouched down in the running water, he felt the cold more, but the sensation remained good as the current washed dirt and sweat from his face and hair and swept most of the dust and dried mud from his pants and shirt. His fingers found the furrow over his left ear, and he was surprised to feel that hair was already sprouting there.

He stood in the stream and scrubbed his face with his hands, feeling good, realizing that whatever had caused his illness a few days ago was gone, and that his full strength and energy had returned. He walked to shore, grunting each time he trod on a sharp stone, and pushed into an opening inside the mesquite cluster. He quickly stripped and twisted and wrenched all the water he could out of his clothing, dressed again, and went out into the fading sun to clean the rabbits.

At that moment, he believed that what he was doing—the quest that now involved Lee—was his job, not a vendetta against the man who'd killed his father. He needed to put an end to Zeb Stone. In doing that, he'd be living up to the oath he'd taken when he became a marshall.

The night was as clear as springwater—the stars were handfuls of carved diamonds spread unevenly on an endless background of black velvet. The slightest of breezes that moved the smoke from the fire was warm and sweet smelling. Next to Ben, Lee gazed into the fire with the same degree of attention she'd give to a book. She explored the embers, watching each whisper of smoke as it was touched and then gently carried away by the breeze.

"I think we're getting closer to them," Ben said. "We'll meet up with the slow route tomorrow sometime, an' then we'll start to see some sign. A big group like that can't travel without leaving a trail, and with Stone and his cutthroats, it'll be even more clear. They'll be just as prone to ride away from a smoldering fire as put it out, an' they'll drop bottles and other junk." He paused. "It'd be good if we knew what town Stone has in mind. I'd like to be there waiting for him and get this thing over with."

"If our first plan works, maybe we won't need the town. Could be that we can harass the gang enough so that they begin to chew on each other—do our work for us."

"Could be," he answered. "I doubt it, though. From what you said, Stone's dead set on a gunfight with me—one-on-one. I can't see him changing his mind."

Lee poked lightly at the coals with a stick, not really paying attention to what she was doing. "You don't have to face him, you know. There are other ways. If we can cause the gang enough trouble, we may be able to take Stone out here, before we even make it to the town."

"That ain't going to happen, Lee. Stone's obsessed. He'll have his gunfight."

A silence that wasn't quite comfortable stretched between them. When Lee spoke, her voice was cold. "You want it too, Ben. You want to fight Stone almost as much as he wants to fight you."

"What I want is to do my job."

She stood up quickly, startling him. "Don't hide behind your job, Ben Flood," she said hotly. "If all you wanted to do was drop Zeb Stone, you could shoot him with a rifle from a hundred yards away. Or you could get some help—Texas Rangers, maybe some of your Pinkerton friends—to bring him in."

"Sounds like you're worried about me," Ben said, grinning.

Her reaction caused him to flinch. "Of course I'm worried about you, you half-wit!" she shouted.

He stood and faced her. "I'm sorry, Lee. I didn't mean to make light." He reached out to her, taking her arm just above her elbow. Her muscle was as rigid as a bar of steel. "C'mon, let's sit down again, OK?"

Lee allowed herself to be guided back to the spot in which she'd been sitting, but where she'd been relaxed before, she was now as taut as a guitar string. "We need to be sure what we're doing—what I'm helping you to do—is godly. If it isn't, we've climbed these hills and eaten rattlesnake and coyote for nothing, and we should head back to Burnt Rock first thing in the morning and forget about Zeb Stone."

Ben hunkered next to her. He was silent for a long moment. When he spoke, his words were quiet, without his usual authority behind them. "Zeb Stone robbed the bank in my town and came close to killing Sam Turner. He carried off and injured a woman who is very important to me. And twenty years ago Stone killed my father. Do I want to punish him for what he's done? Yeah, I do. Any man would. You're wondering if I'm looking for revenge. I hope I'm not. But I won't lie to you. I've been wrestling with whether or not my oath as a lawman covers what I'm feeling. I know this much: Stone is a plague, and I can't let him go on. He'll keep on killing and stealing until he's dead or in a cell. Stopping him *is* my job, Lee." He poked a stick into the fire simply to have something to do with his hands, stirring up a fountain of sparks.

"I believe in you, Ben. I believe you're a good marshall and, more importantly, a good Christian."

"I . . . well, uhh . . ." he sputtered.

Lee smiled. "Oh, hush, lawman. Let's just look at the fire for a while."

The rough bed of the wagon was about as comfortable as a pile of rocks. Discomfort only added fuel to the fire that always burned in Stone's brain. In addition to that, the mules were beginning to fail. They'd had little to eat since leaving behind the murdered peddler and his friend, and their water stops were brief; the men didn't care to spend the time taking them out of the harnesses and then reharnessing them.

"Start lookin' for a place to spend the night," he called to the driver. From where he sat on the side of the wagon, drinking from a bottle of whiskey and smoking a cigar, he motioned to a pair of outlaws who paced the wagon aboard their own horses. "Go on up ahead an' see what you can shoot. I'm right sick of this potted meat—stuff has no more taste than a hunka wood."

Before midday tomorrow, Stone figured, they'd be out of the Backs and headed to LaRosa, maybe a two-day ride. A wide smile spread across his face. He built the scene once again in his mind, as if it had all happened already. His eyes welded to Flood's, the sweat he'd see on the lawman's forehead—sweat of fear—the dead silence in the barroom, the movement of their hands to the grips of their pistols, the heartbeat by which his weapon would clear leather ahead of Flood's, the realization appearing in Flood's eyes as he saw his death sentence being carried out, the crashing, deafening report of his pistol and the metal-to-wood sound when Flood's weapon dropped from his fingers to the floor.

Stone lifted the bottle again, and this time some whiskey flowed over his chin and onto his shirt. He'd been drinking almost nonstop since they'd stolen the wagon. He never got drunk to the point of losing control of his body or even slurring his words, but the change in his mood, his personality, was as obvious as a stroke of lightning on a sunny day. Sober, Zeb Stone was dangerous and unpredictable; drunk, he was a wave of death that struck without reason, its sole purpose to extinguish life.

He lofted the now-empty bottle into the sky and drew, shattering it with a single pistol shot before it began its descent. He stood and walked the few steps to where the wooden case held the few remaining bottles. Moving like a seaman on the ocean, he shifted his weight easily with the erratic movement of the wagon over the rutted trail. He knew the men on horseback were watching him, amazed at his balance after the amount he'd had to drink.

He sat in the place he'd left and pulled the cork out of the bottle with his teeth. He held the whiskey out to the man nearest him, the same man the woman had shamed in the bank in Burnt Rock. "I'll bet that sweet li'l lady's comin' right along with Flood," Stone said as the man nudged his horse forward next to the wagon and accepted the liquor. "Danny, you got any problem with killin' her? See, I don't much care to have anybody alive who puts one of my men on the floor like he was a little kid behind the schoolhouse."

"She didn't—"

"'Course she did," Stone interrupted. "You made the whole gang look bad, gettin' dropped in the dirt by a woman, an' then rollin' around like you was gut shot, whinin' an' carryin' on. Even worse, you made *me* look bad. Tell me this: You ever heard about somebody ridin' with Frank an' Jesse outfought by a woman?"

"I didn't get—"

Stone went on as if Danny hadn't spoken. "You know what Quantrill an' his boys woulda done? They'da strung you right up in the bank from a rafter an' left you twitchin' at the end of the rope for shamin' them." He drank and wiped his mouth. "An' now, you ain't even answered my question. I asked if you were gonna kill that woman—an' I want an answer."

Danny met Stone's glare. "I'll kill her slow. I'll kill her so slow she screams until her voice don't work no more." His voice rose in volume and his words tumbled closer together. "Don't you worry about that. I ain't afraid of dyin'. The only thing I'm afraid of is livin' on an' not killin' that woman." He accepted the bottle from his leader's hand and tipped it above his own mouth.

Stone grinned like a youngster with a new puppy. "Ain't you somethin', boy?" A moment later, he added, "She's all yours. That woman is all yours."

9

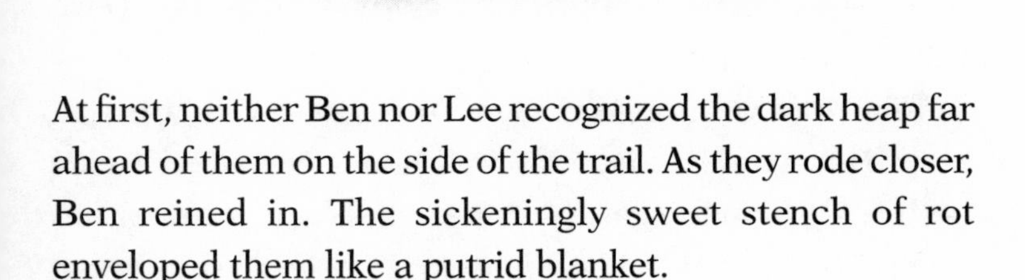

At first, neither Ben nor Lee recognized the dark heap far ahead of them on the side of the trail. As they rode closer, Ben reined in. The sickeningly sweet stench of rot enveloped them like a putrid blanket.

"This ain't gonna be pretty," he said. "That might be an animal up there, but I doubt it. You'd better stay back until I—"

Lee shook her head. "Let's go," she said.

A buzzing, churning cloud of blackflies rose off the corpse and formed into smaller clusters, sniping down at the body erratically but moving away from the approach of Ben and Lee. Ben loosened his bandana and handed it to her. "This'll help a little. Cover your nose and mouth and don't breathe deep." When she started to protest, he held up his hand, cutting her off. "I've done this before. You haven't. Put it on."

Lee looked at the body for a moment and then wrapped the cloth around her head snugly and nodded. They rode the last few yards and dismounted. The horses were nervous at the smell of death; both were wide eyed, and their ears flicked fast, snapping abruptly from one point to another.

"There's another one," Ben said. He led Snorty back from the corpse and swept the area with his eyes. "Must have been drummers—either snake-oil an' patent-medicine hustlers or common carriers of mercantile goods."

Lee swung onto Dancer and walked him past the first corpse toward the second body. After she'd gone several yards, she turned in her saddle.

"There's clothing here, Ben. And tools and nails and . . ." Her voice quivered, and she swallowed twice before she spoke again. "There's dolls and some other toys. These weren't hucksters. They were honest traders."

"Yeah," Ben said. "Lowlifes would've been armed and alert. They'd have dropped a couple of Stone's men before they died. I need to get these corpses underground—and I sure have the tools to do it with."

Lee rode toward a long curve in the trail, following a motion that'd caught her eye. At first she thought it was a bird trapped or caught somehow in the wood of a dead stump—and then she saw it wasn't a bird at all.

"Ben," she called.

He was in his saddle and next to her in a matter of seconds. "What's . . . ?" he began, and then stopped and looked at the stump. Around it, chips and chunks of dried wood were scattered like snowflakes. The Bible, nailed to the stump, was torn apart by bullets, its back cover flapping with the breeze, its pages riddled with holes. The spine of the Bible, probably never the best of bindings, had given up, and sheaves of pages hung precariously, as if the first mild wind would tear them away and spread them over the prairie.

Ben and Lee were speechless for a minute. Then Ben smoothed the remaining pages as best he could and eased the book into his saddlebag. Lee noticed that his fingers were as gentle with the Bible as those of a new mother with her infant.

"Maybe you can see a bit better what I mean about needin' to put an end to Zeb Stone and his gang," he said. His voice was a strange melding of sadness and anger. "You understand now, Lee, don't you?"

"I know what this means. I know that Stone finds it necessary to mock the Word of God. I know that he killed these two poor men. Yeah, Ben, I do understand. Let's get to burying the dead and praying over them, and then ride on." She shuddered slightly and was silent for a moment. "We're getting closer, right?"

"Yeah. The manure around here is maybe a day and a half old. They have the wagon that belonged to the dead men, and it looks like they're trailin' some horses behind it, probably giving them a break from carryin' saddles and men. And see those tracks? They came from mules—

there's no shoes and they have that wide, flat surface mules have. Stone can't be travelin' fast. We can be on him by early tomorrow, if we want."

"That's what I want, Ben," she said. She looked at the corpses again. "These poor men didn't deserve to be cut down like this, and they didn't deserve to have animals and birds tear their bodies apart. I'll help you dig. We . . . we . . . " Her voice collapsed, and the tears she'd been attempting to hide broke loose.

Ben eased Snorty next to Dancer and leaned to her, wrapping an arm clumsily but comfortingly around her.

"It's so bad," she sobbed into his shoulder. "I'm really afraid, but I'm more afraid to let them go on than I am for myself."

He moved back and met her eyes. "We can do this, Lee. I know you're scared—you'd be crazy not to be. But can you hold up? Is this too much for you?"

Lee snorted her nose dry and ran a wrist over her eyes. "There isn't a whole lot that's too much for me, Ben Flood, and you need to keep that in mind."

"I know that," he said. He held her eyes for a moment longer. Then he said, "We can't leave these two like this. There's a bundle of shovels off to the side of the trail up there. I'll get to it."

Lee nodded and glanced up at the sun, checking its position.

"Yeah, I know," Ben said. "If I dig two graves, we'll be here till midnight. The ground is baked and full of rocks. What I'll do is dig one hole big enough for both men. At least it'll keep the animals and vultures off them."

They found a spot halfway between where the two bodies lay. Ben jammed the tip of a spade into the parched, heat-hardened earth a couple of inches and then kicked down on the top of the blade. There was a grinding screech as the steel was stopped dead by a rock. Ben tried again with the same result, and then again—and again. On his fifth attempt, the blade entered the ground without being blocked.

Even when the digging was good, it was bad. The sun drove down like the breath of Gehenna, and Ben's shirt was soon wet with sweat. He worked mechanically at a pace he could maintain, even given the multitude of encumbering rocks that fought against his progress and yielded only when he used every bit of strength he possessed. When dizziness hit him, he dropped the shovel to his side, weaving slightly as he attempted to balance himself. Lee handed him a full canteen, and he drank half of it before handing it back.

"Take a rest. It's my turn," she said.

"You ain't gonna—"

"Don't start with me, Ben! If I can muck out a dozen stalls a day, I can shovel a little dirt." She stepped past him, picking up the shovel, and went to work. When she'd been digging for half an hour, Ben took over again.

Once they were past the majority of rocks, the work became lighter, and the hole's depth increased much more quickly. When he reached five feet, Ben hoisted himself out of the hole and wiped his face with a dripping wet sleeve. He drank deeply from a fresh canteen and sat, shoulders slumped, waiting for his breath to become regular.

"There's one thing I ain't gonna argue with you about, Lee," he said. "Pullin' those men here and gettin' them into the ground isn't gonna be pretty. I want you to stand back when I do it—in fact, I want you to go off a bit with the horses an' stay there till I call you back."

Lee didn't argue. She took Ben's bandana from around her neck and handed it over to him, knowing he'd need it. She touched his face with the tips of her fingers, wiping away some dirt that was stuck to the sweat on his cheek. After a moment she turned away and walked to where the horses were grazing.

When Ben called her back, his voice was hoarse. They stood over the rock-covered mound and prayed together silently. After a few moments, they turned away to their horses and mounted up.

"Not much day left," Ben said.

Lee noticed that he looked pale. "Are you all right, Ben? You look bad. Maybe we should ride on a bit and make camp for the night. I've got a little surprise for you," she said, forcing a smile she didn't really feel.

Ben seemed to weave slightly in his saddle, as if he were suddenly dizzy. "I think that's what we gotta do," he said. "I can't ride like this—my clothes, my hair, my skin all stink of death. Burying those fellas was tough enough, but I can't carry the smell with me." He stood in his stirrups, supporting himself with a hand on his saddle horn, gazing off to one side. "Seems to me there's a little stream off to the east. It's not much, but it's enough for me to wash my clothes and scrub myself off."

"Good!" This time her smile felt real. "Don't you want to hear my surprise?"

Ben grinned ruefully. "One thing I don't need is another surprise."

"You'll like this one. Up next to the trail where I took the horses while you were burying the bodies, I found a five-pound tin of Armor's potted meat. Let's find that stream, and then all you have to do is build a fire and I'll do the rest."

Ben's shoulders slumped with relief, and his smile cut through the dried sweat and dirt on his face. "I don't think I could've hunted down an elephant if there was one a yard away from me. All I want to do is clean the stink off me an' rest."

"And eat?"

"I'm not so sure about eatin'. My stomach's kinda arguin' with me, tell you the truth."

Lee grinned. "Let's get you to that stream. Once you can stand to be next to yourself, you'll eat like a timber wolf in a chicken coop—I guarantee it!"

The right-hand mule stumbled, seemed to catch its balance, and then stumbled again. This time it fell heavily to the left, taking down its equally exhausted partner in a tangle of legs, flailing hooves, and torn leather harness. The wagon wrenched to the left and stopped abruptly as a wheel jammed against a rock.

Stone cursed and spat blood off the side of the wagon. The crashing halt had jammed his bottle against his upper lip and front teeth. He slid off the wagon, spat again, and faced his gang. "Open up on them two useless critters," he bellowed. "An' don' leave nothin' but their fleas in one piece!"

The outlaws obeyed and poured everything they had into the downed mules. The end for the animals was quick, but the whoops, rebel yells, and hoarse laughter of the outlaws continued long after the shooting was finished.

Ben's hide felt wind burned from the scrubbing he'd given himself with handfuls of sand. His hair had already dried and hung limp to his shoulders, where he'd pushed it back from his face. He pulled the slicker a bit more closely around him and picked a final chunk of potted meat from the twig he held.

"I never much cared for this stuff when I had a choice," he mused, "but it sure tasted good today." He muffled a belch with the back of his hand. "Think my clothes might be dry yet?"

Lee walked the few steps to where Ben's pants, shirt, vest, and underdrawers were spread on the ground. After feeling the shirt between her thumb and first finger, she turned each piece over to take full advantage of the steadily descending sun. "Won't be too long," she said. "But we're losing the sun. You'll have to put them on even if they're a tad damp." She held the vest up to her face. "There's no bad smell left, but they're a little muddy."

"Fine with me. I can live with the mud smell and the dampness. I'm sorry, Lee. But it seemed like I was in the grave with those boys."

She sat again next to the fire, comfortably close to him. "There's nothing to be sorry for. It's been a real long day. We both need rest."

"Yeah. We do. I don't think we're a full day behind Stone. Things are going to pick up in a hurry."

She shuddered involuntarily, hoping Ben hadn't noticed. He had. "We'll be OK," he said. "It's a matter of me becoming a sapper, like the sharpshooters at Bull Run. Those men made all the difference in the world. And you're going to be harassing, not fighting."

"I'll fight if I need to."

They watched the sun set without much more conversation. Then Ben stood, wrapped in the slicker, and stepped off to dress in the deeper darkness away from the fire. Lee, half asleep, considered calling it a night and settling in under her saddle blanket.

The crackle of gunfire startled both of them. Lee scurried away from the illumination of the fire and then dropped to the ground, Ben's pistol in her hand. She saw Ben throwing himself to the ground too, his hand darting toward his right holster, which was empty because the pistol that ordinarily filled the holster was still where he'd put it near the fire. The rumble of the Sharp's pealed like a dull, booming bell, and the sharp clatter of pistol and rifle fire continued, as if a pitched battle were being fought over the next hill.

"It's OK!" Ben called to Lee. "They're nowhere near us. The sound carries so clear out here, it liked to scare the pants offa me."

The gunfire continued for a few moments and then stopped, except for a half-dozen pistol shots that sounded puny after the throaty din of the main fusillade.

Ben walked to Lee, extending his hand to her. She faced him and held out the pistol. "I guess you shouldn't get too far away from this, now. Do you think it was Stone?"

"I know it was Stone—and they're closer than I thought." He holstered his weapon. "There's no one in their right mind who'd put that much lead in the air an' enjoy doing it. Did you hear the yells and laughter?" He didn't wait for her to respond. "You need to keep your gun with you every second from now until this whole thing is finished. Stick it under your belt or in one of your pockets if they're deep enough, but make sure you can get to it in half a heartbeat."

She nodded in agreement. "How far ahead do you think they are?"

"No more than two, maybe three, hours. The wagon must've slowed them down. There's no way on earth to get a mule to move faster'n a walk when he's hauling somethin' behind him."

They moved back to the fire. Lee sat; Ben hunkered down next to her. "I guess our days will turn over now—we'll need to rest during the day and do our work at night."

"Except for tonight, of course," she said.

The quarter moon was pale; the hard-edged shadows of late night had not yet arrived.

"Light ain't bad," Ben observed.

There was a pause between them, and it was as if the air itself was charged with urgency.

"My uncle Noah used to say, 'Don't put off until tomorrow what you can do today.'"

Ben grinned in the firelight. "He was a smart man, your uncle."

Lee grinned back. "Let's saddle up. We're wasting time."

The gang wasn't more than six or seven miles ahead of them. Ben and Lee placed themselves in position, using the outlaws' camp as a focal point, and rode toward it.

The first round from Ben's rifle caused an almost volcanic eruption in the center of the still-blazing fire the outlaws had built. Men reached for their side arms and rifles, instinctively rolling, stumbling, or crawling away from the light of the fire. Stone was on his feet, rifle to his shoulder, laying down sustained fire into the darkness as rapidly as he could jack the lever. Pistol shots banged around him, the positions of the outlaws momentarily revealed by the white-orange flame of muzzle flashes.

Ben scrambled away from his original vantage point, keeping low and holding his fire. Bullets ripped through the night air, their sibilant buzzing as frightening as a rattler's warning. When Ben heard hoofbeats pounding toward him from behind, he began firing again until the click of metal against metal told him the rifle was empty. He dropped the rifle, and his pistol was in his hand before the long gun touched the earth. He zigzagged without a pattern, not allowing Stone or his men to draw a bead on him.

Lee rode bent forward, her head inches above Dancer's neck, with the reins in her left hand and the pistol in her right. Dancer seemed to float over the prairie surface, swerving smoothly from one side to the other without a misstep, cued by Lee's knees and lower legs. As she raced past Ben, his form, crouched and feeding shells into his rifle, registered for a fraction of a second and then was swept behind her.

Dancer covered the ground to the gunshot-ridden chaos around the fire like a wraith. The outlaws, Lee and Ben had discovered earlier as they'd watched the movement of the gang, had placed a single man to guard their horses fifty yards away from the fire. Lee saw the vague outline of the animals ahead of her and then, suddenly, the muzzle flash of the guard's pistol. The flame looked big and hot away from the light of the campfire, and Lee swung Dancer sharply away from the burst of light as a slug hissed past her shoulder.

The outlaw fired again, and again she heard hot lead whisper past her. She fired twice toward the outlaw, not bothering to aim. His third shot responded almost immediately, and she quickly understood that this man was not only sober and alert, but he was also aiming each round toward what he could hear but not quite see. A bullet tugged like cold, probing fingers at the hair held in a shaggy bun at the top of her head. She threw another unaimed round toward the outlaw and hauled Dancer into a collision course with the flashes from the man's weapon.

The cold nugget of fear that had stirred in her stomach with the first shot now grew to an uncontrollable, arctic chill that launched a shiver throughout her body and sent electric tingles to her limbs. The curses and shouts of the outlaws and the barrage of bullets became to her a mélange of fear and death, and she felt as if she were being dragged through the gates of hell. Dancer missed a stride at the same moment that a burst of yellow-red light flared, followed by a blast of thunder that attacked her like a living thing.

Dancer went down on his left shoulder, and shards of bone and blood slapped Lee's face like an unexpected burst of hard rain. She kicked out of the stirrups a moment before being slammed against the dirt and scrub of the prairie. Her breath whooshed out of her, and she rolled like a flung rag doll. Both her nostrils began spewing blood. A second ball of light exploded, and she swung her pistol toward it just as the ear-shattering report reached her. She fired two shots rapidly, by instinct, and a quick, high-pitched scream started and stopped within the same second.

"Lee! Are you all right? *Lee!*"

She struggled to her feet, gasping for breath. Ben hollered "Behind me! Swing up behind me!" at the top of his lungs, and she heard hooves pounding toward her above the continuing gunfire of the outlaws. Snorty swung past her to her left, stretched to a full gallop and turning tightly around her.

"Swing!" Ben shouted, but she already had her arms clamped around his waist, demanding that Snorty's juggernaut momentum carry her up and onto his back.

"We've got to get you a horse!" Ben hollered.

She pointed to the left of where the outlaw had stood. "There! Go!" she demanded, and then, "Wait! Stop! I need my hackamore!"

Ben hauled back on the reins and dragged his horse to a sliding halt. Lee was off Snorty before he was completely stopped, and she ran toward the dark form on the ground that was Dancer.

Tears seared her eyes as she tore the hackamore from Dancer's destroyed head, his blood warm on her hands. She took a quick moment to stroke the dead horse's neck, and then Ben and Snorty were by her again. She grabbed Ben's waist and was behind him on Snorty as if the short break in time—the time in which she'd said good-bye to a horse she'd come to love—had never occurred.

Ben aimed for the center of the group of horses that were tethered along a lariat attached to the wagon at one end and the wooden shaft from the mules' harness rig at the other. Lee pushed off Snorty's back as Ben swung away from her toward the campfire. She heard him firing as she stumbled along the line of snorting, wide-eyed horses. A gray, taller than the animals on either side of him, caught her eye. She ran her hands quickly over his back—no saddle sores—and across his chest—good width, decent muscle, but thin, sharp ribs. She untied the line from his halter to the tether. In a moment the hackamore was over his muzzle. Grabbing a handful of mane, she hauled herself onto his back and jammed her heels into his sides. Whether or not he'd been trained to a hackamore, he'd be sure to understand what a quick punch in his side meant.

Lee rode her new mount hard, the balance and skill she'd built up over the years keeping her welded to the horse's back. She stuffed her pistol—still clutched in her hand as if it were an extension of her wrist—into the deep pocket of her skirt. The gray handled himself well; he was agile and quick around obstacles she couldn't see until she was past them. But she could feel him failing. Even an animal with heart couldn't sustain a hard run without the benefit of decent feed.

Where is Ben?

Lee checked her horse's run, unsure if he was responding to the hackamore or if he was simply unable to continue the headlong gallop. His wheezing told her he was very tired, but the taut muscles of his chest and behind his withers promised he'd go on if she demanded he do so. Easing him into a jog and scribing a wide circle, she ended up facing in the direction from which she'd come. There was no more gunfire, but she heard hoofbeats coming toward her. Her pistol was empty, and the cartridges Ben had given her were in Dancer's saddlebags.

If it was one of the outlaws coming after her and she called to him or even gave some sort of signal, she'd be dead in seconds. But if she didn't call out and it was Ben, he could ride right past her and continue searching for her until it was light. She couldn't let that happen. She and Ben needed rest badly, and the mount she'd just stolen was not far from caving in.

She let the galloping horse draw closer and then yelled out, "Ben! Over here!" Almost immediately the rhythm of the hoofbeats changed tempo and turned more directly toward where she sat on her exhausted horse. She closed her eyes and prayed for deliverance if the approaching rider was not Ben Flood.

When he called out to her with panic in his voice, she answered with another yell. He was beside her in a moment. He took her into his arms from atop his horse, and she leaned into his embrace from her mount. Her body shook almost spastically as she clung to him. Once the tears began, she choked and coughed and let them flow, knowing there was no way she could stop them.

"You let a Bible-thumper an' a woman raid the camp, an' you didn't get either one of them—an' then you let them steal one of our horses?" Stone sprayed saliva as he ranted. He began pacing rapidly through the group of men, who parted as he approached them, giving him plenty of room. None of them met his eyes; they knew better than to do that.

"What happened to the lookouts? Where's that useless baggage Charlie, who was supposed to be watchin' the horses?" He glared at the men. "Charlie! Charlie, git over here an' face me like a man!" He moved a few steps closer to the fire.

"Charlie, he caught a bullet, Boss," a voice from the group said.

"Dead?" Stone demanded.

"Yeah. The Sharp's is all busted up too. The slug musta hit it an' blew it up in his face. He was on the ground, an' he—"

Stone yelled and threw up his hands in despair, cutting off the outlaws with his motion, as if he'd received the worst possible news he'd ever heard. The men looked stunned. Their leader never reacted to death—anyone's death—in such a manner. Gang members had died in robberies and barroom gunfights, and Stone himself had killed more than a few of them, but he'd never paid any more attention to a bloody death than he would to stepping on an ant.

Stone stood for a long time, looking down at the dirt between his boots, not speaking. The men looked increasingly more nervous, as if this was a side of their leader they'd never experienced. Finally, Stone broke the tense silence.

"My Sharp's is wrecked. That voodoo man busted up my Sharp's."

They sat at the side of the stream they'd left a few hours earlier. False dawn was creeping into the sky in the east. Lee was shaky, feeling hollow, as if the life had been drained from her.

"I hit the man, Ben. I fired at him and I hit him."

Ben waited a moment before answering. "You had no choice. He was tryin' to kill you. He'd just killed a fine horse tryin' to put a bullet in you. He was shootin' at you with the most powerful rifle ever made."

He stood and faced her, reaching down to lock his hands on her shoulders and forcing her to meet his eyes. "You didn't set out to kill that man—an' you don't know for sure that you did kill him."

"He's dead. When I went back to get my hackamore, his body was still there—right where he fell when I shot him."

Ben released Lee's shoulders and hunkered down next to her, taking her hand. "Let's pray," he said gently. Lee swallowed hard and then nodded.

"Lord," he began, "we're right up against it. We need your help and guidance more than either of us ever has before. Your daughter Lee may have taken a life in what we believe is a just and righteous quest. She ain't a killer, Lord, an' I know you recognize that. I ask you to come to her now and make your divine presence felt—an' send her away from here an' back to Burnt Rock if that's what's best for her. The responsibility for what happened last night is mine, not hers. I shoulda never let her—"

"Please, Ben, don't," Lee whispered, her head still bowed. She prayed to herself silently. Then she forced all thoughts from her mind and let herself become completely open to God's counsel. Almost immediately, her shoulders relaxed and the cold knot in her heart eased. She felt warm and whole.

She didn't realize how tightly she'd been hanging on to Ben's hand until she released the pressure. But she didn't open her eyes yet.

"I acted on my own when I demanded to come with you to stop Stone's gang," she said. Her voice was low.

"Pray for strength and speed, Ben, and ask that the Lord protect us as we go on—together."

After a moment, Ben continued. "We ask your help, Lord. We beg you to ride with us, that you keep your hands on us as we do this thing that we believe must be done. Amen."

When a long moment of comfortable silence ended, he stood and stretched. "You gotta get some sleep now. I'll be back in a couple of hours."

"Back? Where do you think you're going without me?"

Ben grinned. "I ain't gonna have you ridin' that saw-back you picked up last night without a saddle." He held up his palms to her as if to stave off the tirade he knew was coming. "I know, I know—you learned to ride bare-back as a kid an' you're just as comfortable without a saddle an' all that. Thing is, I don't care. I want you to have some leather to grab if you need to. You get some rest."

"Rest? How in the world do you think I'll be able to rest? You think Stone will hand over a saddle if you tell him we're one short?"

"He will if I ask him nice an' polite. You get some sleep, OK?"

Ben headed off at a lope, Snorty working well under him and covering ground quickly but without undue exertion. He was sure Stone's gang had moved on, but nevertheless, he drew rein a good mile from where he estimated Dancer's corpse to be and went in that direction on foot. He scanned the prairie in all four directions as he walked, ready to throw himself to the ground if Stone had set up an ambush. Above him, buzzards were gathering, swinging lazy quarter-mile-long ovals in the sky, their harsh *screee!* the only sound that reached his ears.

Ben looked at Dancer as little as possible as he unfastened the girth and tugged the saddle off the dead animal's back. The left stirrup was under Dancer's side, and Ben dug in the dirt with his hands before using all his strength to haul the stirrup and fender free.

The large group of buzzards had separated into two distinct flocks of fifteen or twenty each. One cluster was circling over where the outlaws' camp had been, while the other stayed above Ben and the dead horse. Ben set the saddle aside, wiped sweat from his face, and strode to where the gunman would have been standing. It was impossible to miss the location of the body; the vultures were beginning to descend in twos and threes.

From where he stood, Ben saw both the body and the singed barrel of the Sharp's rifle split its full length. The lever mechanism of the buffalo gun was angled upward, blown and twisted from its original position by the explosion of Lee's bullet striking the firing chamber. The stock was splintered and blackened.

Ben stood looking at the dead outlaw longer than he needed to. The corpse's left arm was extended, and the hand was a perfect thing, its fingers curling easily toward the palm.

He collected the saddle and walked back to where he'd left Snorty.

10

There were too many of them, and they were riding too fast for him to lead them with his rifle. Their gunfire was constant, one report part of another so that it sounded as if a Gatling gun was trained on his and Lee's camp. Bullets whined past him like tiny comets, striking rocks and careening off into the night with high-pitched screams.

She was standing with his pistol in one hand and the rusted, broken weapon she'd taken from the dead outlaw's saddlebag in the other, firing at the riders. Their slugs spit past her face, touching her hair and her clothing. He yelled at her to get down, but she didn't seem to hear.

Now her guns were empty, but she continued pulling the triggers. He worked the lever of his rifle, and the mechanism stuck in midstroke. As he tugged at it, the metal stretched like still-warm taffy. At the same time, the blued-steel barrel drooped toward the ground, hanging from the wooden stock like a length of old rope.

She was still standing, but now she was crying, choking out heart-wrenching sobs that hurt him more than any outlaw bullet would have. She was calling to him, gasping his name, but he couldn't move. The barrel of his rifle had wrapped itself around his boots, and his upper body was numb and lifeless, as if his limbs were no longer attached to him, as if they existed somewhere far away from him. She called again and again . . .

"Ben! Ben!"

Someone was shaking his shoulder. He screamed again, his legs kicking and his body writhing. He opened his eyes and stared around, wide-eyed, without really seeing, his mind spinning with the images and the raw fear of the dream. He pulled a sleeve across his sweat-drenched face and attempted to speak, but his tongue was stuck in the dryness of his mouth. He swallowed to generate saliva and then croaked to Lee, "I'm OK. Jus' a bad dream."

"It must have been real bad. I was sound asleep, and then I heard you scrambling around in the dirt. I didn't know what to think."

Ben stood shakily, looking for his pistol in the stingy light of the new moon. He found the gun ten feet away, where apparently it'd been kicked as he'd thrashed around.

He remembered going to sleep with the tips of his right fingers touching the grips.

Lee moved to his side. "Want to tell me about it?" she asked softly.

He shook his head. "Doesn't warrant telling," he said. "Kid stuff is all it was."

He picked up a stick and poked at the small fire they'd built earlier in the day. He'd killed and cooked a rabbit, and then they'd slept the day away in the sparse shade of a cluster of mesquite and desert pine.

"I had kind of a bad one too, during the day," Lee said. "About Dancer and how he went down."

He nodded. "This whole thing is gonna give us bad dreams for a while." After a moment, he added, "We better get ready to ride. I want to get those men to the point where they're afraid to see the sun start to go down 'cause of what they know is coming when it does."

"They'll have more guards posted tonight, won't they?"

"That's the thing. We have no way of knowing what Stone will do. Any normal man would double his lookouts, maybe even have an outrider circle the camp all night. Maybe he'll do that. Maybe he won't. It's like tryin' to guess which way a scalded cat's gonna run."

"What can we do, then?"

Ben gripped her hand for a second, and then released it. "Nothin' says we can't be crazier than they are."

There were two fires, about fifty or so feet apart. Even from where they sat on their horses a couple of miles out, Lee and Ben could see the orange-red tongues of flame.

"I've got an idea," Ben said quietly. "We can't hit them like we did last night, and we got to assume they have at least a couple sober lookouts around. What I need you to do is hold tight until you hear shooting, and then ride in closer and put as much lead in the air as you possibly can. Don't get within pistol range. Afterward, you ride hard this way. If we can't find each other tonight, we will in the mornin'. An' remember what I said about stayin' out of range. Hear?"

"But suppose—"

"No supposin'. You do like I say this time out."

Lee began to speak, but Ben put his hand on her shoulder, silencing her. "We ain't got time for this."

"I don't even know what you plan to do!" she protested.

"I'm pretty sure if I told you what I'm up to, you wouldn't like it much. You got to trust me a little here. OK?"

She nodded, and then, not sure if Ben had seen her head move in the darkness, said "OK."

Ben leaned to his side from his saddle and kissed her. She was surprised by the kiss, and he seemed a bit surprised too. But it was very much welcome. Her hand found its way to the back of his neck. He moved his mouth from hers and put his face next to her head. Snorty shifted his rump a bit, and the two moved apart.

Ben clucked to Snorty, and the horse took a stride away from the gray Lee was riding. "All set?" he asked.

"Yes," she whispered.

He tapped Snorty with his heels, riding off to one side, away from both her and the fires. She set her horse ahead at a walk, the pistol in her right hand and the reins in her left. After a few yards, she stopped, reached back into her saddlebag, and removed some cartridges. She placed six of them between her lips, holding the bullet ends lightly between her teeth. She could hear the light drumming of Snorty's hooves, and she cringed each time one of his shoes struck a stone; the ringing clanged in her head like an alarm bell.

Ben reached into his saddlebag and whispered a quick prayer of gratitude that Nick had loaded him up so well with ammunition. There wasn't much light, which was both good and bad. The outlaws would have more trouble seeing him and Lee, but, on the other hand, the floor of the prairie could be dangerous—fatal—at a gallop. The risk, he decided, was one he had to take.

In less than an hour, he was behind the fires, watching the flames reach into the sky ahead of him. As he jogged Snorty closer, his shoulder and back muscles tensed; he could almost feel the cold blue rifle sights moving with him, past him, and then back to him as an outlaw tracked him by sound and eased the trigger back.

The first round struck a rock twenty feet to his right and ricocheted, its scream like that of a banshee. Then a cacophony of rifle and pistol reports tore the night apart. Ben swung Snorty back and forth in wide arcs at a full, breakneck gallop, making his path impossible to predict. The fires rushed toward him, and he saw dark shapes moving rapidly past the flames.

Snorty was as strong as a locomotive as Ben drew close enough to see that some of the outlaws had their backs to him and were firing away from him. He threw a pistol shot at a man with a rifle standing in front of the left fire and saw a quick spit of dirt about four feet in front of the outlaw. Ben raised the muzzle of his pistol a few inches and squeezed the trigger twice. The rifleman went down.

Ben dragged Snorty into a sliding right turn and then into a left, placing him on a course between the two fires. A slug soughed by his shoulder, touching his sleeve as gently as a mother's touch, and another geysered dirt a yard in front of Snorty. A fat man swung a rifle toward him and then fell to his knees as Ben fired by instinct, without aiming.

The fires were much closer now—twenty yards—and then ten in a heartbeat. Ben aimed at an outlaw and squeezed the trigger. The hammer fell on a spent cartridge. He holstered the gun and took a wrap around the saddle horn with the ends of his reins, leaving Snorty enough slack to continue his run. Then he reached into the pockets of his vest.

Lee counted her shots, firing first toward one fire and then the other, keeping her horse at a fast lope. She took a wrap around the saddle horn with her reins and pushed the cylinder of her pistol open with her thumb, letting the spent cartridges drop free. Then, taking them one at a time from between her teeth, she fed in six fresh bullets. She clicked the cylinder closed, freed the reins with her left hand, and turned her horse back in the direction from which she'd come. She was close enough to the pandemonium near the fires to hear the curses and yells of the outlaws as they fought against their unseen attackers.

She was much closer to the outlaw camp than Ben had wanted her to be; it was her decision, she believed, and she'd opted to come into the action, where she could do the most good. A bullet whispered past at chest height, and another buzzed over her head. Again she counted her shots. She placed two rounds toward what appeared to be a cluster of three or four outlaws, then fired two more at a muzzle flash. Her fifth round went directly into the fire, scattering bits of burning wood into the air. She shot at another muzzle flash and then tucked the pistol into her pocket and slowed the gray as she reached back to her saddlebag for more ammunition.

Strangely, the sharp click of a hammer striking a cartridge reached her ears over the almost-constant gunfire from the camp. Then, immediately, she heard a hoarse, guttural string of profanity and felt a body slam against the side of her horse. Strong, hard hands were wrenching at her left arm and shoulder, attempting to dump her from her saddle. Her weakened horse stumbled under the impact but caught his balance.

Lee clenched her fist and swung hard at the face of the outlaw who was now almost in her lap. The sweat on the man's face glistened in the light from the fires, and her breath caught in her throat. It was the outlaw she'd floored during the bank robbery in Burnt Rock. She swung again and again at his face in a panicked frenzy. His eyes, embers against his skin, radiated pure hatred.

The gray, confused and beginning to panic, moved clumsily, not allowing the outlaw to get his feet under himself steadily enough to use his weight and superior strength to haul Lee down from her horse. The man bettered his grip, still cursing, one arm over her lap and clenched over her right leg, the other dragging at her left shoulder. Her fist skidded across the sweat-slick face without much effect until she punched his nose with a fear-generated strength she didn't know she possessed.

Blood gushed from the man's nostrils in torrents, spattering her clothes and face. But his grip didn't loosen—instead he boosted himself almost across her lap. The fetid, hot gasps of the man's breath gagged her as she continued to pound at his face. She screamed and grasped a handful of his thickly knotted, greasy hair and did her best to wrench his head backwards.

But her strength was nothing against the bull-like muscles of his neck. The man was double her weight and was fueled by unadulterated hatred. She let go of his hair and jammed her right hand into her pocket in search of her pistol. Even though the weapon wasn't loaded, she could use it to batter his face. But his hold on her leg made reaching the gun impossible. She struggled to get her fingers around the bone grips, strained to wedge her hand under the gun. It was futile. *Dear God, please . . .*

The tips of her fingers touched the flat surface of the piece of knifelike stone she'd found days ago. She screamed again and pulled the stone free. She clutched it in her fist and swung the weapon in a vicious arc across the outlaw's face.

The blade gouged down the length of his cheek from beneath his ear to below his jaw—and then it pierced flesh and seemed to sink away from her hand. The outlaw's eyes flared as he opened his mouth to scream, but he was only able to bring forth a wet, gurgling sound. He released his grip and fell away, striking the ground on his back. She looked back at him. Both of his hands were moving toward his throat. She brought her horse under control and raced out into the darkness.

Ben bent forward at the waist, his hands clutched around as many cartridges as each would hold; two from his left hand escaped and dropped to the ground. The fires were within yards of him, and then within feet. Fewer bullets sought him out as he barreled toward the opening between the fires, guiding Snorty with knee and leg pressure, urging yet more speed with his voice.

Clusters of men gaped openmouthed at him as if he were an apparition; a few stopped midmotion. Ben straightened in the saddle and pitched a handful of bullets into the fire on his right. The fire to the left was too far away to reach with an offside pitch. He used his right hand to pull Snorty into a sliding stop and then rolled the horse back over his haunches and hurled him back toward the fire. As his horse scrambled into a gallop, he twisted in the saddle and dug both hands into his saddle-bag, filling them with bullets and then clutching them tightly at his waist.

The outlaws were no longer stunned; lead screamed past him, the slugs seeming as thick as a cloud of angry wasps. He kneed Snorty into a collision course with the fire and prayed for more speed. He could see the men's faces clearly now, as well as the barrels of rifles belching fire and the muzzles of pistols flashing quick bits of whiter light. A bullet slammed the cantle of his saddle. Another round gouged a long furrow across the top of Snorty's rump, and another smacked Ben's left stirrup, jarring his boot loose.

Then Snorty was in the air, launching over the fire, the flames licking greedily at his sweat-drenched belly. He and Ben were weightless for a moment, floating, and then were captured once again by gravity.

Ben opened his hands and let the cartridges cascade into the conflagration. For the smallest part of a second, his eyes met with those of Zeb Stone, who was standing in a half crouch, his mouth pulled back in a lupine snarl. Ben knew their battle would be to the death—the clashing of their eyes sealed the violent pact. There was no going back, and he didn't even want to.

The bullets in the right fire began exploding as Snorty dug away from the camp. Outlaws sprinted away, running awkwardly, their shoulders hunched and chins tucked.

The crackling of shots and the screams and yells of the outlaws fell rapidly behind Ben as Snorty carried him away from the melee. The cartridges exploding in the fires had a different sound than those fired from the guns—a sharp *crack!* rather than the deeper voice of a shot muffled by the chamber and barrel of a weapon. In a few moments the ammunition in the fires had done its work, and the only gunfire Ben could hear was a random round. Those too ended in another few moments.

Ben rode hard, putting space between himself and the outlaw camp. He doubted the outlaws would come after him, but he wouldn't swear to anything where Zeb Stone was concerned. After a while, he brought Snorty down to a slow lope, letting his mount carry that gait for a good distance before reining him to a walk.

Then he drew rein and dismounted. When his fingers moved over Snorty's rump and down his flank, the horse flinched and took a quick step backward. Ben's fingers came away with a thick wetness on them. He lowered his head to Snorty's skin and peered closely where his fingers had touched. He cringed when his eyes picked out a foot-long channel carved into the hide and muscle of the horse's right flank. He found another, shorter furrow low on Snorty's rump.

Neither wound seemed to be bleeding badly, but both were open to the air, and flies would be a problem the next day. He moved to Snorty's head and rubbed his hands up and down the dripping horse's muzzle, still speaking softly to him. He tugged the bandana from around his neck and used it to wipe down his mount's chest and sides. Snorty grunted with pleasure, his breathing rapidly returning to a normal pace. When he snorted almost thunderously, Ben figured his partner hadn't suffered any long-lasting ill effects.

Ben too was coming down from the massive wave of adrenaline that had carried him through the assault and escape. The images, sounds, and smells of the battle washed over him; he could feel slugs reaching for him, touching his clothing, hissing past his ears. He shook the thoughts away and instead focused on Lee.

But pictures once again flashed through his mind—far more frightening pictures than those of before. Lee being shot from the back of her horse. Lee slamming into the dirt and rocks. Lee screaming as half a dozen desperados dragged her up from the ground . . .

He shook his head violently. *I told her to stay out of range. She'd do that—she'd obey me. She knew how important it was that she stay out of pistol range. She wouldn't . . .*

But he knew she would.

Ordering Lee Morgan to do something was like ordering a hawk not to protect her nest. Ben searched the darkness around him, looking for her. He loosened Snorty's girth, grabbed the reins, and walked ahead of the horse. After a hundred yards he passed his hand under the saddle. Snorty's hide was cool, and his breathing was slow and normal. Ben mounted up as the sun was peeking over the black line of the horizon.

They weren't much more than three hundred yards apart when they saw one another. Two tired horses galloped toward each other across the prairie in the seething heat of the direct sun, and Ben and Lee were out of their saddles and into each other's arms.

They soon found a small oasis where the stream that cut through the prairie—the same stream they'd bathed in a few days earlier—formed a shallow pool. Ben shot a prairie hen and a fat blacksnake and built a fire, not bothering to conceal the smoke. Lee took Snorty into the pool and washed him down with the tepid water, sluicing it over his wounds and inspecting them carefully, looking for any sign of infection or any bit of foreign matter. She then mixed a paste of soil, water, and bits of reddish clay from the streambed and applied it thickly over the gouges in Snorty's hide.

They didn't speak much as they set up their camp and made preparations to sleep through the day until it was time to ride.

"We gotta get this over with soon," Ben finally commented. "I need to get some coffee." When Lee failed to respond, he asked, "What happened last night?"

"What happened," she said carefully, "is that I'm sure I killed another man. He had hold of me and was trying to pull me out of my saddle. It was the man I hurt back in Burnt Rock, in the bank. I had a piece of shale, I guess it was, that I picked up a while ago. My pistol was empty. I stabbed him in the neck. He let go of me and fell back. Then I rode away." She put her head in her hands.

"I'm sorry that happened, Lee." He waited for a moment and then went on, his voice a bit louder. "But if you'd stayed out of range like I told you to, it wouldn't have. Stone wouldn't post men out that far—they'd be useless in an attack on the camp. You were in close enough so that this thug could get his hands on you."

"Yes."

"Why didn't he shoot you? He must have—"

"His gun was empty—jammed or empty," she interrupted, her tone matching his. "I heard the hammer strike before he grabbed me."

"You shouldn't have been there! I told you—"

"I know what you told me, Ben. And you might care to remember this: I'm not your wife, and I'm not subject to you!"

Ben wrestled with a smile for a moment. "I've noticed that," he said. "A married man wouldn't be shiverin' under a saddle blanket all alone at night if he had his wife with him."

Lee blushed for a moment.

Ben poked at the dying fire, and the moment was gone. "It'll be over soon," he said. "I'm real sorry you were put in a position where you had to protect yourself again. The only thing I can tell you is what I said before. Your cause is a just one."

"I know that." She fell silent, and tears filled her eyes. "But I can't just forget what's happened. I've taken two lives, and I'll never be able to wash the blood from my hands, not for as long as I live."

"All the more reason for you to head—"

"If you tell me that I should leave you now and go back to Burnt Rock, I'm going to thump you a good one! That's a settled issue!"

Ben smiled. "Feisty today, ain't you?"

Stone yanked his horse's head around and jogged back to regroup his gang. The outlaws, down to nine men, slumped in their saddles, their shirts and vests soaked with sweat. Several had rags or clothes wrapped around their arms or legs, blood seeping through the soiled fabric of the shirts taken from those killed during the raid of the night before.

"You men are ridin' like a bunch of squaws bein' run by the cavalry," Stone snarled. "Right as you sit there, you each got more money than you ever dreamed of havin'. You gonna let a Bible-thumpin' voodoo man an' a city woman take it away from you an' run you off like a buncha sheep? Is that what you cowards want?"

None of the men met his eyes. He wrenched his horse into the midst of the loosely clustered desperados. "I'm gonna tell you this again: We ain't stoppin' till we ride into LaRosa. We're gonna go through the night an' we're gonna go through the day till we get there. If a horse drops, that man walks if he can't get a ride on somebody else's crowbait, an' we ain't slowin' down none for him either way. We'll divvy up the money soon's we hit the town. We're gonna take over that place like we own it. After that, any man who wants to head out can go ahead an' do it. Any who want to ride with me are welcome to stay on. After I kill that marshall, I'm headin' deeper into Mexico. There's lots of places that ain't even heard of us yet, an' it's a sure bit they ain't ready for us."

Stone jabbed his spurs into his horse's sides and jogged ahead, turned, and faced the men. "I held back two quarts of whiskey. We'll pass the bottles till they're empty.

If anybody else is carryin' whiskey, git it out an' pass it around." He added as an afterthought, "I'll kill any man who drops out or tries to break away before we git to LaRosa."

He took a quart bottle from his left saddlebag and tossed it toward his gang, following it with the quart from his right saddlebag. He gave them ten minutes to pass the bottles and spoke again. "You want to watch me gun the marshall, that's fine with me. Maybe you're thinkin' it won't work out the way I want it to, and the lawman'll kill me. 'Fact, you're probably hopin' that's the way of it. It ain't gonna happen that way, but you're free to come an' watch the show." He spat on the ground next to his horse. "Let's git to it. We got some ground to cover."

The clouds that had obscured the moon the night before had been whisked away by a brisk breeze that came up while Ben and Lee slept away the heat of the day. The wind had died by the time they saddled up, but the cold front behind it dropped the temperature to an October level. Lee's gray wasn't much good for any gait beyond a lope, and that for only short periods of time. Snorty, however, invigorated by the change in the weather, tugged at his reins and crow-hopped a few times to show his rider he was tired of the dull pace.

"This boy is gonna drive me crazy," Ben said. "I need to let him out a bit to get his edge off. If Stone stops about the time he usually does, we'll be on him before too awful long. Maybe I can catch a look at their camp—see where they're vulnerable."

"But he'll have lookouts tonight. Maybe we should stick together."

Ben shook his head. "I'm afraid you're runnin' out of horse. That gray is tryin' his best, but he probably hasn't had decent care in a year or more. It's better I go on ahead, an' you hold to a walk an' save what he's got in case we need to run for it."

Lee touched the outside of her pocket, feeling the hardness of the grips of her pistol. The double handful of bullets she'd loaded into the pocket offered a reassuring weight against her leg. "You're right. I'll keep moving as fast as I can without killing this poor animal." She looked around, turning in her saddle. "I'm not sure of the directions."

"Just keep them two stars—see that one an' then the one below it?—off to your left, just like they are now. I'll be back in two, maybe three hours. It's hard to tell how much ground Stone might've covered."

He reached out to her, and she took his hand and held it. Neither spoke. When Snorty tugged at the bit, they loosened their grips. Ben turned Snorty away and gave him some of the slack he'd been holding.

It was a good night for riding. The moonlight was soft and shadows were deep, but the rocks and depressions in the prairie floor were obvious enough that if Ben missed seeing them, Snorty didn't. Better than two hours out, he reined in next to a shattered whiskey bottle that had caught the moonlight. Shards and bits of glass glinted like fresh snow some distance around the largest piece of the bottle. It had been used as a target. In another half hour, he came upon a second bottle, and then a third. He slowed Snorty to a walk, scanning the land ahead of him. He squinted to pinpoint a fire and strained to hear a curse or a yell. There was nothing.

That didn't make sense. The outlaws always stopped at dusk. Why would they change their ways now? An ambush wasn't logical, not with Stone's obsession with killing him in a gunfight mimicking the one they'd had before.

He stopped Snorty and sat thinking, unsure of what to do. He'd told Lee he'd be back in a few hours, and that much time had already gone by with no sighting of a camp or any other activity. If the gang hadn't stopped, and if an ambush wasn't in their plan, what were they up to?

The answer hit him like a punch to the gut. *They ain't goin' to stop—they're goin' right in to LaRosa. It must be LaRosa, or they'd have swung off by now and headed west to the next nearest town. They're riding until they reach their destination, and LaRosa must be it.*

He knew Lee would keep on coming whether he returned or not. Maybe he could get the whole thing over and done with before she caught up to him. Maybe he could finish Stone before she even reached LaRosa.

He dismounted and filled his hat with water from his two canteens. Snorty drank thirstily. Ben finished what water remained, checked Snorty's girth, and ran his hand over the paste Lee had used to coat the wounds. There was no heat on or around the gashes. He mounted and clucked Snorty into a lope.

The painted plaster head of the statue of the Virgin of Guadalupe exploded when Stone's bullet hit it, putting a thick cloud of heavy, whitish dust into the humid air inside the church in LaRosa. Stone's horse, skating on the polished wood-plank floor, upset the outlaw's aim; his second shot missed the statue completely. He cursed and then laughed as the Madonna disintegrated in a shower of grit and painted particles of plaster. He emptied his pistol at a pair of smaller statues set on either side of the altar and dragged his rifle out of its scabbard. As he was working the lever, his mount's rear legs skidded apart and its rump slammed into the floor. Stone stepped out of the saddle as the animal struggled to rise. He turned the rifle on the animal and put a round in the side of its head. Then he exited the church and headed out to the eerily empty streets of LaRosa.

As he strode out of the church, a wooden table was hurled through the plate glass window of the cantina across the street, spewing a fountain of glass splinters. Rifle and pistol fire seemed to be coming from all sides, accompanied by drunken whoops, rebel yells, and the racket of furniture and glass being destroyed.

Stone stood outside the saloon. One of his men raced by on the back of a sleek but panicked Appaloosa. He was spurring the horse cruelly and grappling drunkenly with the reins. Stone raised his hand in greeting and watched, laughing, as the horse suddenly veered into the open front of the town blacksmith shop and stable. The cross beam of the barn caught the outlaw in the face and ripped him off the horse's back.

Stone chuckled to himself as he entered the cantina and plucked a bottle from behind the bar. He drank from it and chuckled some more as he watched his men stumble in and out to fetch whiskey. He hadn't yet reminded the gang about the girls' school just outside the town; he was saving that for after he'd bested Ben Flood.

He took a final drink from his bottle and then tossed it out into the street. The whiskey tasted good, but he could wait for more of it. He didn't know how close Flood might be.

Ben heard the rattle of gunfire long before the town of LaRosa popped up on the horizon. He'd ridden through the night and well into the next day without rest beyond periodic stops for water. Now the sun was beginning its descent.

He knew he should feel more tired. But even after almost eighteen hours in the saddle, his mind was clear and his reflexes were keen, as if electricity flowed through his body. He reined in and dismounted, then took the small can of gun oil from his saddlebag and worked a tiny drop of it into the action of his pistol. He checked each cartridge and replaced one of the five with a fresh bullet. The thin thong holding his holster to his leg had loosened; he untied it and brought it up snug. He dropped his weapon into his holster and let it settle there. He didn't bother to draw—it was too late for practice. Either he was or wasn't faster and more accurate than Zeb Stone. He'd know for sure within a few hours.

And he knew Lee hadn't stopped since he'd left her, unless the gray had given out. If the horse was still carrying her, she would be several hours behind him. *Just as well,* he thought. *I'd rather meet her as I'm riding out of LaRosa, if that's the way it's going to go.*

A fresh burst of gunfire erupted from the town ahead of him.

A series of pops muted by the distance reached Lee's ears. Her back was stiff from hours in the saddle, and the wind that had started that afternoon began to chill her as it continued to sweep in from various directions. But the gunfire chilled her more than the wind; she had no way of knowing whether the bullets were directed at Ben. She'd prayed all night and through the day until her mind had gone blank and her entire world consisted of the weary horse taking one stride after another.

She heard another cluster of shots.

Snorty pushed scraps of brown prairie grass with his nose, looking for clumps worth eating. Ben forced himself to sleep for an hour or so while he awaited full darkness. But even though he was able to relax his body, his mind churned with quick pictures of Stone drawing on him, of Lee riding toward him, of where he might be the next day.

He's going to die, she thought. *It's just like Uncle Noah told me. When a good horse has reached the very end of his bottom, there's a surge of life that comes to him, that pushes him like a strong wind from behind, to carry his rider farther and faster until the end comes and the horse dies proud.* Even though the darkness and the drop in temperature had seemed to invigorate the gray, she felt him weave under her and drag his hooves—a sure sign of exhaustion. Her uncle had ridden a horse to its death to save his own life once, and he'd told her of the experience. He'd cried at the horse's courage and heart. Now, Lee cried just as her uncle had.

The sole light in the town of LaRosa spilled through the smashed window and batwinged entrance of the cantina. Ben rode down the middle of the street at a walk, the hairs on the back of his neck and arms standing stiffly. He worked his shoulders to ease the tension from his muscles, wondering how many guns were trained on him at that very moment. He knew Stone wanted the fight too much to allow an underling to gun him, but there was always the possibility that a tequila-fueled outlaw would take matters into his own hands.

A man lurched drunkenly out of the cantina, looked down the street at Ben, and hustled back in, slamming the batwings.

Now I'm into it, Ben thought. *There's only one way out now.*

The voices and laughter from inside the cantina stopped. He watched the flicker of the lanterns as the wind struck them. The light inside would be fairly good, but he'd need to let his eyes become used to it before he encountered Stone. He dismounted and ground tied

Snorty across the street from the cantina, feeling the weight of eyes on him as he started toward the building.

A zephyr blew grit into his face, and he used his right forefinger to wipe his eyes clear. Tears started as he blinked, and he impatiently brushed them away with the back of his hand. He stood to the side of the entrance with his eyes closed for a long moment. There wasn't a sound from inside; the silence seemed as threatening as that of a firing squad before the final command was given.

"Thy will be done," Ben said loudly enough for those inside to hear. Then, stepping in front of the doors, he eased his eyes open and pushed through into the saloon.

His mind scrambled to sort through the images as he walked into the room. A man passed out on the floor in front of the bar, shards of glass in the frame of a destroyed mirror, men along the side wall in chairs, most of them with bottles in their hands—and Zeb Stone, standing at the far end of the bar, under one of the four lanterns set in a line the length of the room.

"Ain't gonna be *thy* will, Flood. Gonna be *my* will."

A calmness settled over Ben—a gentle breath that blew away tension and fear. The electricity was now focused in his right arm and hand, but it was a pleasant sensation, paradoxically easy and restful. He could somehow move his hand and raise his arm without using his body.

He looked at Stone, whose eyes were glinting like pools of crude oil reflecting bright sunlight. For a moment, the hatred in them weakened Ben's strange sense of tranquillity.

Stone moved forward, stopping a dozen paces from him. "Voodoo ain't gonna save you this time, Flood. You ain't gonna cheat me like you done twenty years ago. This time you're goin' down to stay."

Ben shifted his left foot back a few inches. His right hand hung loosely at the end of his arm, his fingers curling inward the slightest bit toward the grips of his pistol.

A drunken outlaw accidentally elbowed a bottle off the edge of a table, and the sound of it smashing was as sudden and unexpected as the blast of a cannon. Neither Stone nor Ben flinched.

"Man who done that's gonna die," Stone promised.

Ben watched Stone's right shoulder with his peripheral vision. Usually, a man's eyes would reveal when he began his move, but Stone was too good to let his eyes betray him.

"You don't have to do this," Ben said calmly, still keeping his eyes trained on his opponent. "There's another way."

"Ain't no other way. Can't be no other way, lawman."

"Think for a moment, Stone. Do you want to die in this lousy cantina in front of a bunch of scum who'd love to see you dead? Do you really want to end your life right now, with the weight of so many sins crushing you?"

Stone's shoulder dipped, and his palm slapped the grips of his pistol. His draw was clean and breathtakingly fast—the arc of the barrel swung upward flawlessly like the flashing head of a rattlesnake, all deadly speed without wasted motion. When the barrel of his pistol was level, he screamed.

He was being lifted off the floor by an unseen force. His weapon deserted his hand and crashed against the back wall of the cantina as two of Ben's bullets ripped into his chest. Then he was on the floor.

Ben crouched and swung his smoking pistol toward the outlaws along the wall. "We're done, Marshall," one man whispered. "We got no reason to fight you." He stood slowly from his chair. "You got no jurisdiction in Mexico. We're leavin'—ridin' out right now. You got no reason to gun us." He turned slowly, stiffly, and walked to the entrance. He stopped for a second, shoulders hunched as if expecting a bullet, and then pushed through the batwings and into the street. The others followed until the cantina was empty except for Ben and Stone.

When Lee burst through the batwings a moment later, the muzzle of Ben's pistol found her instantly, and the hammer began its trip back. He wrenched the gun upward as it fired a round into the ceiling. She ignored the blast and ran to him, throwing herself into his arms after he dropped his pistol into his holster. Her tears were wet against his face, and he could feel her trembling.

Stone groaned. Ben tensed and whirled away from his embrace with Lee, shoving her out of the line of fire. But there was no need. Zeb Stone groaned again.

Ben and Lee walked over and crouched next to him. Blood ebbed from the holes in his chest, and more from the exit wounds in his back pooled around him.

His eyes met with Lee's. There was confusion—and fear—in his unfocused gaze. The horrible flames that had lit his eyes earlier were quickly running out of their foul fuel.

"Ask Jesus to help you," Lee whispered hoarsely. "Ask him to be your—"

Stone's mouth opened as if he were going to speak. His throat constricted, and he struggled to push out a word. Then his eyes closed, and his mouth gaped open. Lee touched her fingers to his cheek for a moment and then slowly moved them away.

Ben stood and eased Lee up by her hand.

"Did we do him any good, Ben? Did we . . . ?"

His voice was weary and hoarse. "I don't know. I hope we did. But I don't know."

She searched his eyes. "It's over. It's finally over."

Ben gathered his woman to him and held her, but he didn't trust his voice enough to speak. He had a lot to say, but he'd get to that later.